MW01258913

shit-head

the american dream
high school sports and
perceptions of reality

felix rush

ISBN: 978-0-9816009-3-2

WWWWW
WWWWWW

1 2 3 4 5 6 7 8 9 0

N

Contents

Frame of reference

Stepping out from behind the veil of over a dozen pseudonyms, Felix Rush continues to view the world from a perspective that only a person of his incomprehensible background could realize.

A product of the foster care network, Rush lived in fifteen homes before his twelfth birthday, at which time he was permanently assigned to a juvenile detention center for repeated petty crimes. Although small in stature, he was often found at the center of skirmishes that, more times than not, left him in the infirmary for extended stays. Uninterested in communicating with his peers, he was ultimately transferred to a psychiatric hospital at the strong recommendation of a staff psychologist who feared for his safety.

At fifteen, Rush would finally have his first full year of formal education, where tutors discovered that despite his tendency to go weeks without speaking, possessed a deep understanding of the English language. Unable, or unwilling, to engage in any subjects outside the creative arts, he would divide his time between writing, playing the guitar, and digesting the Internet. Convinced that he possessed an extraordinary intellect, several instructors began the process of untangling his stories that were often found intermingled among his nonsensical drawings and doodles, many times bouncing between the numerous languages that he had taught himself online.

In his early twenties he was moved into an apartment complex adjacent to the hospital that was intended for transitioning patients back into society. Shortly after, Rush first became involved in rewriting texts under the careful eye of his appointed guardian. Over the years he developed into a mainstay in the artistic world, with creative focus in both literature and film. Still preferring to communicate on paper rather than through speech, his ability to identify proposals with critical appeal, or completely transform a piece of work, have made him one of the most sought after people in the business.

As an editor of countless manuscripts, he has been known to consume five hundred pages in a single day, or take an entire month to examine a lone paragraph. On occasion, there is also the added inconvenience that he has been known to return only the burned ashes of manuscripts that he didn't like to the author, regardless of their fame or past success. However, for those not too proud to receive their works covered in red ink, profanity scribbled across sections and covered in coffee stains, his creative genius is unparalleled.

Which brings me to Shit-Head, the first work that he requested be put out under his given name. The entire script was presented between the lines of several newspapers two years ago, and it took nearly eight months of work to make sense of the story that was written in seventeen different *languages, including an entire chapter written backward in Hebrew.*

It has been my pleasure to work with Felix over the last twenty years and provide the funnel through which he reaches out to the rest of the world. Working as editor, psychologist, legal guardian and friend, I am excited to have been a part of this project. Created from his unique observations of life, and presented in an unprecedented format, it is a true reflection of his considerable abilities.

Elizabeth Hill

Prelude

Academics, researchers, marketers and scores of others have gone to great lengths overanalyzing the innumerable reasons people across the globe have logged onto the Internet in logarithmically exploding numbers since becoming accessible to the masses. Although the original driving force was for educational and technological reasons, more times than not, it is the interpersonal facets that have attracted users and kept them coming back time and time again. For all the hype written concerning how it's changing business, education, and formal communications in general, in a society where the pace of life is accelerating out of control, it is the basic need of individuals to simply find someone to talk to that is driving its growth, and more significantly, ensuring its future. It is simple, inexpensive, and in real life terms, only a 'click' away.

Those with obscure interests or oddball personalities who rarely, if ever, find confidants among those they run across through traditional interfacing, find an endless array of individuals lurking throughout cyberspace with similar propensities, abilities and peculiarities. The geek or nerd is suddenly the center of attention in the chat group, while the captain of the football team is struck with his insignificance where the physical realm is no longer relevant. These fundamental shifts in the basic interpersonal roles that had remained unchanged since humanity learned to communicate, now often lead to relationships that prior to the Internet would never have been possible.

Thus, the setting for this story. A friendly relationship that started between two surfers who had never met each other face to face. After several months of bumping into each other in a variety of chat rooms where they shared common interests, they began to correspond regarding their work. One a counselor, the other a struggling part-time private investigator trying to launch his business. It was their common desire to work with other people, and the reality that they both had nothing better to do than spend most evenings online, that brought them together with a most unusual personality, and an even more unique set of circumstances. A man searching for a single answer to a peculiar question led Steven (pistevo), Robert (bertco2), Dr. Lisa Cochran (imdoc), and eventually many others through his bizarre upbringing and unique surroundings that had somehow failed to destroy him, despite everyone's best efforts. They would find themselves challenged with a seemingly simple task, which turned out to be irrevocably tangled with the demons that had haunted an entire community for three decades. Solving their seemingly simple assignment would ultimately involve an elaborate attempt to rewrite history — or at least everyone's perception of it.

STEVEN

S t e v e n
stood looking out his front picture window, sipping a cup of cold coffee and contemplating the future; which in his case, generally meant reflecting on the past. He wasn't sure why the second anniversary of his divorce left him so depressed. He had realized from the beginning that his ex had been an irrational choice, and the dissolution had ultimately proved a great relief to him. If he wanted to be honest with himself, he had realized even while they were still dating that it was a doomed relationship. The only real mystery had been how, or why, they had managed to stay together for nearly five years. His friends claimed that they had been concerned about her from the onset of the relationship — which might have been convenient insight before they were actually married. Thankfully, there were no children, and the split had been as amicable as such things can be. Once the formalities were over on that dreary afternoon, she had jumped into a car with a vaguely familiar man, headed south out of town, and he hadn't seen or heard from her since.

Somewhere down inside he was aware that it wasn't the sense of loss from the marriage, but the loss of the last two years that haunted him. At the time he had been able to convince himself that his new freedom would finally allow him to follow his dreams; whatever that meant. A promising grocery store manager, he seemed destined for corporate management. The advent of the superstore had resulted not only in his long-time employer closing their doors, but also his subsequent employer. Now, his career had managed to slide backward into merchandiser at a mega-store that offered little upward mobility, substandard pay, poor benefits and no sustainable level of interest. However, they did have a nice cheerleading session for all employees each morning. He cringed at the thought and drained his cup.

Painfully aware of his limited future, at least he could credit his marriage with making a somewhat warped contribution to his life. After paying a private investigator $1,700 to tell him what he, and apparently everyone else already knew, he had taken an online program to get his own license, which he had managed to obtain a few months back. The only missing piece was anyone willing to pay for his services. That was until last night.

He moved away from the window, poured another cup of coffee and flipped on the weather channel. He unconsciously rubbed his right knee and sat down, the lingering effect from knee surgery a year earlier as a result of an adult basketball league injury. It was a fitting end to his less than illustrious athletic career. He had tried to follow in his older brother's all-conference steps, but after riding the bench in his freshman and junior varsity years, the varsity coach mercifully cut him. Ten years later his brother had invited him to join his recreation league team, which after three thoroughly humiliating performances, ended with him landing awkwardly while trying to block a shot, and three weeks later undergoing the knife. His new athletic goal comprised of turning the injury into an excuse for permanent retirement from anything resembling a sport.

He glanced at his watch, sighed, dumped out the rest of his coffee into the plant next to the couch, and headed out the door for the morning cheer session. Tonight, Robert would be online and he could bounce the strange tale of his perspective client off him. A little professional perspective was probably in order. It didn't seem like much of a case, but at least it would give him something to distract his thoughts throughout the day. More importantly, it was a case, a real case, his first case.

ROBERT

Wednesdays

were Robert's 'court appointed' days. Thirty-minute sessions with a counselor, some weekly, some monthly, few worthy, mandated by the State. He was the only member of the office that drew a full eight hours, the unspoken right of passage he had assumed as the youngest member of the staff. From what he could tell, none of the other counselors had more than an hour a week dedicated to the State. They claimed it was invaluable training. He had quickly come to realize that it was a hard lesson in reality for everyone entering his profession that not all clients have any interest in seriously addressing their issues.

When he had selected social work as a career, a number of his friends had warned him that the mental strain of dealing with an endless parade of life's difficulties, presented on an hour by hour basis, would harden even the most idealistic. However, that had just made him more committed to the cause. Now, it wasn't necessarily the difficulties, but the sameness that wore on him. Not that every situation didn't have its own twist, but the ongoing sense that in most cases there was so little real help that he could offer. Everyone from the client, to their family, to the State, was constantly in search of a fast, painless solution to complex issues that had typically taken a lifetime to create.

Then, there were Wednesdays. The day when not only was he left feeling helpless, it was a stream of clients that didn't want to be there, didn't think that they needed to be there, and sincerely had no interest in anything that he had to offer. It was a case of both client and counselor glancing at their watches every few minutes as they labored through the session. His paying clients struggled to include every possible detail, relevant and not, into their appointed time, often making it difficult for him to provide adequate responses. On Wednesdays, the primary task was trying to coax more than yes or no answers from the clients in an often futile effort to minimize the dead space.

He pulled the file of his first client from the cabinet. Heather had dropped out of high school, was a budding alcoholic, the daughter of alcoholic parents, had been abused by her uncle, beaten up by her last boyfriend, had lost her daughter to the courts, spent time living on the street, arrested for drunk and disorderly, DUI twice, petty theft, possession of marijuana, and finally driving on a revoked license. Assigned to Robert, she was particularly distressing because he honestly liked her. He looked down at the folder; she would turn nineteen in two days. His assignment was to straighten out her life over six thirty-minute sessions.

He glanced at his watch — five minutes, if she bothered to show up at all. He knew what bothered him most about Heather; it was Jane, his fiancé. He had seen so many women with abusive pasts, and regardless of what successes they might enjoy in life, the abuse seemed to linger, and Jane was one of them. It was something that remained in the back of his mind with every case like this. Jane was clearly an 'overcomer.' She had made it through the dark years, confided in her aunt, with whom she lived when her mother refused to believe that her third husband could do such a thing. She attended the obligatory counseling, finished high school, honors in college, and was now in her second year of dental school. She had even managed to confront, and forgive, her parents. Something Robert instinctively knew that he would never do. He simply didn't want to, and had come to complete peace with his position. For the life of him, he couldn't imagine why Jane had chosen him.

Heather snapped him out of his trance as she stumbled into his office, obviously drunk. It would be a good night to talk to Steven, a person that he had never met in person, but had developed a close friendship with after offering a free piece of advice in an office sponsored chat group when he was going though a divorce. Steven seemed to find the lighter side of everything, and even at this early hour, Robert could tell that by the end of the day he was going to be in the mood for something lighter. Heather suddenly stood up holding her stomach, he had seen the look before, she was about to be sick right there in his office – again.

DAY ONE

SEPTEMBER 8ᵀᴴ

5:23 p.m.

pistevo: I had one of my more unique visits from a potential client yesterday morning.

bertco2:   Not to be confused with the other two you've had since setting up shop last spring I presume?

pistevo: Abuse accepted. Now, if you can possibly ignore my feeble attempt at running a business long enough to hold off on the sarcasm, I'll try to move my tale along.

bertco2:   Fair enough.

pistevo: A rather strapping man, that's the only way I can think to describe him, came into my office, which as you know is also my house, with what seemed to me a somewhat bizarre request. He claims that regardless of where his life has led him, and there have been a variety of geographic and ideological changes through the years, the name Shit-Head has somehow always managed to follow him. Now in his forties, with a young wife and an infant son of his own at home, it has suddenly become of some interest to learn where this rather auspicious title first originated, and what is more important, how it has managed to follow him regardless of location or circumstances. Once that part of the sleuthing has been completed, he would like to permanently separate himself from the name if possible. Although I'm not certain where to even start in a case such as this, I suppose that the answer has to be somewhere in his youth. Being the shrink that you are, I rather thought you might find a sort of professional curiosity about such an unlikely assignment.

bertco2: I've had many patients throughout the years who struggled with names or nicknames. Everyone gets tagged with less than kind titles throughout life, particularly during the cruel childhood years, but certain individuals take them to heart, and it's not as rare as you might think that they leave lifelong scars. Most of them tend to focus on some sort of physiological flaw or oddity in the individual's appearance or mannerisms. As a result, they become a constant reminder of their most sensitive deficiency. On occasion, I have even treated patients who have had a fixation on an illusionary name or title. Although, normally

I would expect to see this more in line with illusions of grandeur rather than self-deprecation. However, if the patient has tendencies more toward paranoia......... I would suggest that you start with whoever is closest to him now. You mentioned that he had a child. I would start with his wife, significant other, or whatever else you might find sleeping around the house.

P.s. I'm not a shrink, I'm a counselor. That means I see all the people who can't afford one, and probably couldn't be treated by one.

p.s.s. Are you going to get paid for this job?????

pistevo: Yes, I'm going to get paid! Can you believe it! Let's hear it for P.I. correspondence schools!!! Actually, this guy seems to have all kinds of money. He owns the patent on the Clean Kids Shower Device that allows young children to get clean while they play in the tub.

bertco2:   I hate to admit it, but I think that I'm familiar with the product, and no, I don't own it.

pistevo: Their great claim to fame is that, allegedly, no parental oversight is required during bath time. You simply screw on the attachment to your shower head, fill it with some of their proprietary soap, naturally available only through their company, and for the first five minutes your child is rained down upon with an environmentally safe mixture of soap and water that is guaranteed not to cause eye irritation to your precious child. The following five minutes, soap free water rains down and rises off the tot. Upgrades include a patented chamois to better clean for $19.95, a patented shower curtain for $29.95 that is guaranteed to keep all the water in the tub, patented pads in case junior falls for only $39.95, and even a suction cup mounted camera for only $49.95 (he couldn't get a patent), so that the committed parents can watch both TV and their child. Predictably, you can't purchase any of their products without signing the five page disclaimer. They advertise it as quality parenting without the burden of being in the same room as your child. One of their catch slogans is, "don't let their bath time interfere with your plans."

bertco2:   I've been called on to council a number of parent –child issues. Regrettably, my experience has proven that there is a large market for helping family members avoid any real interaction, and I suspect that many parents will pay handsomely for the service.

pistevo: He claims that several years ago he was tiring of the corporate life and exploring options to start a business of his own. He was at the age when several friends had young children, and the one common thread that they all shared was a desire to be good parents. However, in equal measure, they seemed to lack any genuine desire to invest any 'real' time in junior. To his trained marketing eye there seemed to be an enormous opportunity in developing products that made parents feel as though they were being attentive parents, regardless of their actual contribution.

bertco2: That would be the market I was referencing. The only challenge would be to find a way to access them without letting on that you're mocking them.

pistevo: They do all of their sales through late night infomercials. He claims to have about seventy-five people working for him in some small town that I've never heard of about fifty miles south of Toledo. They have had to slow down the advertising rotation as of late because they are generating too much business for the company to manage. He claims that he's working seven days a week to try to expand the company into what he amusingly describes as the endless market of 'parents who like to pretend that they care.'

I have to admit I don't know much about him at this time, although it seems odd that he went to the trouble to track me down. I'm not exactly blessed with a long list of satisfied customers. Apparently, a web page can make anyone look like more than they are. He insisted on driving over to my house, but our appointment lasted for less than twenty minutes, and he spent the whole time glancing at his watch.

bertco2: I've seen that many times in my practice. Generally, that means that eventually you will learn that someone else, probably his wife, insisted that he pay you a visit. Any chance that you're listed first in the phone book.

pistevo: No, but now that you mention it, I am at the top of the second page of one book.

bertco2: Sorry to be the bearer of reality, but the proximity of your ad on the page probably had more to do with being selected than your impressive resume.

pistevo: I can live with that. I'll take a paying client any way that I can get one. I'm on the run now; I have a meeting for my 'real' job. I'll post a note as soon as I learn anything new. Say hi to the wife and kids.

bertco2: No wife, no kids. I thought you knew that?

DAY THREE

SEPTEMBER 10TH

5:24 p.m.

pistevo: You won't believe this. I finally tracked down our client's wife and she referred to him as SH! Claims that she was introduced to him by a friend about four years ago. She said it was nearly three months later before she learned that SH stood for Shit-Head. She thought it was some kind of stupid macho nickname he had picked up in college until they traveled back to Michigan to meet his mother shortly after announcing their engagement. She was stunned when his mother referred to him as SH, and worse yet, everyone else in the family; uncles, cousins, etc., all referred to him as Shit-Head just like they were calling him Bob or Mike. She seemed quite upset by the whole thing. She fears that if the name persists, it will leave an irreparable scar on their child. Her exact words were, "How is a son supposed to show respect for his father when the entire world refers to him as Shit-Head?" And they say that quality parenting is dead.

bertco2:   I'm sure Dr. Spock would be proud. It sounds like you have a great case on your hands my friend. His wife refers to him as SH with the misguided assumption that their son will never figure out what the initials stand for. Even if it was something different, it would be Shit-Head when junior was fifteen years old hanging out with his friends. How about his real name, did she ever consider calling him by that? For that matter, has anyone considered using his real name? At the risk of being unnecessarily simplistic, that seems like a reasonable alternative to a profanity-based name. As for the rest of the family, I probably wouldn't feel compelled to visit anyone who insisted on addressing me as Shit-Head. I assume that your client, who is beginning to sound more like a patient, does have a real name, doesn't he?

pistevo: Ah, his 'real' name — I agree that would be a reasonable alternative, however, that's where it gets even more interesting. His given name, and yes I'm being straight, is Abraham Lincoln. It seems his mother was born in Illinois and had a fascination with a particular historical figure.

bertco2:   Why am I not surprised to learn we have a bizarre fixation rooted in this family? No wonder he was in his forties before he began to question his common name. His given name probably would have started even more fights on the playground growing up. Are you getting paid enough to go spend some time in his hometown? Sounds like this could be an interesting group to meet with for a few drinks down at the local tavern.

pistevo: I'm leaving tonight. The opportunity came up yesterday, so I jumped on it before I could even get your thoughts.

bertco2: I find that the answers to most issues are typically nearer to home and family, rather than farther.

pistevo: I get three days a year that I can take off for personal reasons. That, coupled with my usual time off, gives me a week to spend in the U.P. I'll check back the evening of the 12th at 5:00 p.m. to update you on what I've learned, if anything. Is that a good time for you, or should I just put it in your box?

bertco2: If possible, I'll meet you online on the 12th. By the way, what is the U.P.?

pistevo: The Upper Peninsula of Michigan. I'm heading up into the frozen tundra. I know it's only September, but the weather turns bad early up there some years, so I'm hoping for the best. I'm told to expect little more than trees, and then more trees on the drive up. Should be an interesting trip. Until later.

DAY FIVE

THE U.P.

SEPTEMBER 12TH

5:17 p.m.

pistevo: Are you out there?

bertco2: Here and waiting. I was afraid that your plans had changed and you were going to be a no show.

pistevo: Sorry I'm late. It's been an incredibly insightful day. It took me several hours this afternoon just to find a place where I could sign on. It seems this part of the world is a bit less wired than I have become accustomed to. The first motel I stopped at was such a bargain that not only don't they have wireless, they don't even bother with phones in the rooms. Although, they do have a satellite dish out front that can pick up ninety-nine stations, about half of them porn. Let me start by admitting that I'm well beyond my professional abilities with this case; where should I start?

bertco2:   How about at the beginning. Just start with your trip and ramble on. I've got all evening. One of the many disadvantages of Jane living two hours away. I can pretend that I'm too consumed with my profession to bother with trivial matters, when in reality I'm just socially inept without her.

pistevo: All right, but I think you're going to have a hard time believing some of this. First, do you know how far up here it is. It took me seven hours after I reached Motown! As I was warned, there are trees and trees and more trees broken up by the occasional gas station and party store. You can drive for miles and miles without passing another car in the other direction. On the positive side, the speed limit appears to be something comparing to the Autobahn. I was doing eighty, yet on several occasions was passed, or more accurately, blown passed by young men in 1985 vintage Ford pickup trucks, who sccmcd gcnuinely irritated that my leisurely pace was causing them delay.

bertco2:   Obviously, they had important places to be.

pistevo: One can only imagine. On the drive up I had a lot of time to think, and came to the conclusion that the best place to start might be at the local high school. Not only did it seem best, I couldn't come up with any alternatives. I wanted to get some background on both Abe and his family before I started snooping around the ole' stomping grounds and tracking down whatever family that he has remaining in the area. I was hoping some of the teachers might still remember him. Even though it has been many years since he left, being that it's such a small town, I was naively hoping that just about everyone knows everyone.

bertco2:   That's how this business typically works. You just keep following every nugget of information you manage to dig up, and hopefully, they lead to somewhere meaningful. There is more effort than intellect involved in most cases.

pistevo: After winding through a maze of hallways that seemed to follow no rational pattern, I entered the high school office where I was greeted by a young lady who couldn't have been any more than twenty years old; she may have even been a student. With so many women trying to look twenty, it's difficult to tell these days. Being a bit road weary, I walked up and inquired if there was anyone around that could provide me with some background on Abraham Lincoln. It wasn't until it popped out of my mouth that I realized how ridiculous the question must have sounded.

"You need to go see Coach Reed. He mentored Shit-Head all the way through school and probably knew him better than any. Though, I don't 'spect there's anybody in these parts that still keeps in contact with him."

I was only half listening because I was instantly struck that it had never even crossed her mind that I might be referring to the historical figure! She knew exactly of whom I was inquiring, even though she couldn't possibly have been alive when he left high school. That was just my first indication that SH carried a much larger legacy in this small town than the real, or more accurately the first, Abraham Lincoln. It wouldn't be the last time!!!

bertco2:   Sorry to interrupt, did your young receptionist show any signs of emotion when you mentioned that you were inquiring about good old Abe?

pistevo: Feel free to jump in anytime, it may keep me from needlessly rambling. Regarding your question, as odd as it seems, there was no emotion, no surprise, no anything. She simply answered my question as she banged away at a letter on a manual typewriter while noisily smacking on her gum. Any thoughts?

bertco2:   Nothing for now, just a slightly vague note to tuck into my mental file for later. So, did you manage to get an opportunity to talk with Coach Reed? If he was one of Abe's coaches in high school, there was a good chance that he would remember him.

P.s. Did you actually mean a manual typewriter???!!! Sounds like they're preparing our children well for the future!

pistevo: Ah yes, a throwback to yesteryear. The two electric models weren't just for filling out forms, they were the technological centerpieces of the office. There was cutting edge technology on display throughout the office. For a moment I feared I had slipped into some kind of time-space continuum. However, when I finally managed to locate Coach Reed's office, I found him sitting behind an Apple iMac with a twenty-inch screen. He was playing golf, and quite proud to point out that there were only two kids in the entire school he couldn't consistently beat, and that was only because, as he put it, "they just sit around all day smokin' pot and playin' golf, while I have a career and family to tend to."

bertco2:   That's how he introduced himself?

pistevo: That was it, he never even told me his name. It was straight to the video golf enlightenment. Did you know that most courses favored the player who has perfected a controlled slice?

Coach Reed

5:21 p.m.

pistevo: How shall I do justice to Coach Reed; late fifties, a badly managed comb over, 5'7", 195 lbs., thick neck — he looked like a bulldog, even his facial features. Tragically, exactly what my imagination had conjured up during my short walk to his office. Loud, intense and completely out of touch with everything going on around him. The poster child for if you can't do it, coach it. Until our meeting, I'm not sure that I fully appreciated what that generalization truly meant. It's crystal clear now. I was so intrigued by our conversation that I took detailed notes. He spoke fast, but repeated the same things over and over, so I think I got most of it down. To add to the entertainment value, I'll try to capture the dialogue if possible.

bertco2: I would appreciate it if you could capture everything in dialogue. It helps me to get a much clearer picture of the people that you're dealing with. Personalities tend to reveal themselves more when people are speaking in their natural tone and style.

pistevo: No problem, I brought along a recorder that I can keep out of sight to help ensure that I get my notes correct. Marginally ethical, I confess, but I'm not trying to deceive anyone, just make up for my personal note taking limitations. I'll try to feed you everything verbatim. Now, back to Coach Reed.

"So, you say you're tryin' to dig up some dirt on one Abraham Lincoln. Well, you've come to the right man in this town, yes sir. You some kind of cop or reporter or something like that?"

"No, no, I'm doing some investigating...."

"Say no more, say no more," he held both hands out and closed his eyes in a way that contorted his entire face. "I'm always happy to cooperate with the authorities. Just promise to send the article when it's done. I don't subscribe to no papers or magazines, ya know there's powerful forces influencing what's reported, can't get the truth there. The best info is on talk radio and the regulars down at Dino's Bar. Those two sources and you can dang well figure out most things," he tapped the side of his head with his index finger as he spoke.

bertco2: What a big surprise. You can't imagine how many 'Coach Reeds' I've counseled through the years. Admittedly, most without success.

pistevo: "Now, back to Abraham Lincoln," he enunciated each syllable like he was a southern preacher. "That sons-a-bitch cost me big time. I mean **BIG** time. People round these parts call him Shit-Head ya know, but not me, that be a label too good for that low-life snake crawlin' kid. I hope he's in trouble, I mean big trouble," he started to rise up out of his chair. "When I got him expelled from this school back in the spring of 1978 I told him I would pray every night for the rest of my days that he failed in the game of life. Ya know, that's one promise that I've kept, and to this day I still feel just as strong. Get all sweaty just talkn' 'bout it," he slammed his fist into the desk and knocked over his can of Coke.

"What did he do? I mean, for you to still carry all of this rage around almost thirty years later isn't healthy." I was trying to be helpful, and had no idea what an appropriate response might be.

"More than just to me you understand, he did damage to this whole frickin' town for generations. The students, the parents, the kids, for years to come were all ripped to pieces by what Abe did that spring afternoon. Damn, my grandma would still cry about it over a beer with me up to the day she croaked out on the back porch. Shoot, the night she bit it last spring we'd been carryin' on about Abe for hours. I thought she was just all choked up, didn't even notice she was dead for nearly an hour. She always looked that way when we talked about him, I only got tipped off something was wrong when I noticed her beer spilled over. Granny didn't do that lest something was wrong, and I mean dead wrong," he shook his head as he spoke, failing to catch his own slightly morbid irony. "What Abe did is still talked about most nights down at the pool hall. We've been replaying it in our minds endlessly since that day. I dare say it's frickin' consumed this once fine town. Better put, he damn near destroyed this town."

I'll break from the dialog with Coach Reed for a minute to try to gather my thoughts. By this time you can image that there were all kinds of things running through my mind. What kind of hideous thing could a senior in high school do that would completely paralyze an entire town for three decades? Yet, from my research on Abe, albeit of marginal quality, I wasn't aware of anything even slightly questionable about his past, and this mystery event would have taken place after he was eighteen, so anything serious should have been a matter of public record. His biggest crime to society seemed to be those cheesy low-budget infomercials that constantly pollute the airwaves in the middle of the night. How could he have done something with such long lasting repercussions, and yet, at least by appearances, never been punished for it? Did he rape the prom queen and get away with it? Run over a little kid while he was drunk? Back to my notes.

"What did he do?" I was finally able to break into his diatribe when he paused for a much needed breath.

He paused for a moment, obviously trying to organize his thoughts, "He missed *the* throw," it was all he could do to spit out the words.

"He missed a throw?" Not a very clever response I admit, but it was all that I could think of at the moment since my expectations had been mounting in such a different direction.

"Yeah, *the* throw mind you, not just any throw," he seemed truly offended that I had referred to it as *a* throw rather than *the* throw. "Eighty-seven percent from the line and he missed the most important throw of this sorry town's frickin' history," he pounded the desk again, spilling what was left of his drink as he stood up and peered out the window behind his desk.

"He missed *a* free-throw?" I admit that, somewhat childishly, I emphasized *a* again. "You're pissed at him because he missed a free-throw in a high school basketball game?" I realize that I should have sounded stunned and appalled, but I think my tone came across in a monotone that appeared disinterested.

bertco2: Sounds like he's got a great grasp on life. Maybe you should give him my number, this guy could need years of counseling, and I can always use the business. Patients like that who have a steady income are difficult to find.

pistevo: I would like to tell you that was as bad as it got, but regrettably, it continued down its slippery slope.

Coach Reed calmed down a bit, brushed his hair carefully back into place, slid into his chair as he tried to gather himself, and then continued with his story much like he was delivering a sermon. "Picture the scene; it's March 1978, the stands are packed and we are playing for the Michigan Class D State Championship at Jenison Field House, East Lansing, Michigan," he managed to completely separate each word as he slowly spoke. Obviously, it was the same speech that he had been giving around town for the past thirty years. "The very building that would become home to one Erving Magic Johnson that very fall. Ya know, I lifted this from that sacred place as a memento," he suddenly broke from his trancelike speech and picked up the folding chair that he was sitting on. "No small task, I might add," he returned to his seat and closed his eyes in an effort to recapture the mood of the moment. "One year later the same Magic Man and Greg "Special K" Kelser, would shut down Larry the Bird-man and the ISU Sycamores to win the National Championship, on what remains to this very moment, one of the highlights of my entire life. I mean this was the big time," his eyes suddenly popped open and I dropped my notepad on the floor.

"Anyways, we're playing St. Martin in a rematch from the year before where I successfully brought home this town's first State Championship in its history. First ever, any sport, any time. I was *the* man in this town." We were back to emphasizing *the vs. a* just in case I still hadn't caught on. "You appreciate that St. Martin is a power," it was part question, part statement. Clearly, he was starting to doubt a flatlander such as myself truly understood the complete significance of the spectacle at hand.

"I mean football, basketball, class D, class C, they were the frickin' power to be reckoned with in this state. Even though we'd busted their arses on the same floor the year before, they were ranked ahead of us in the polls all season, and took the floor with a swagger that told us we had no business even showin' up at the gym. They treated last year like it was some kind of frickin' freak accident that didn't count, and they were gonna prove it over the next two hours," he told the story like a proud parent still defending his jilted child.

He pushed away from his desk, leaned back, and put his hands behind his head as he stared up at the ceiling and continued with his tortured tale. "It's tip-off, and we've won fifty-three straight games. Do you hear me, fifty-three straight games! We *were* this town!" He glanced down at me for a moment. "I mean parents got discounts on the cars they bought, parking tickets werc ripped up without question — why we even bought a team bus from the mayor's frickin' budget. Cost a janitor his job to recoup the dollars, but hell, it was a one owner vehicle." I could see that he was flashing back to a moment that I was desperately hoping to avoid learning more about. "I could get a teacher fired for givin' one of my boys a D, frickin' union or not," he had shifted positions and now had both fists on the desk leaning out toward me as the veins in his neck stuck out. "Even riding the pines was worth at least one grade point. We were about to go big time in this town in ways that truly matter. One more State Championship and we were gonna add a department to the school budget where fathers of promising fifth and sixth graders from other towns could be janitors, at a very generous wage I might add, while their sons balled here. It would have virtually guaranteed us being a powerhouse for years to come. We would have become the next St. Martin. U.P. power baby!"

bertco2:   At least he had a plan.

pistevo: Not for just the school, he had big plans for himself as well.

"People everywhere in this state would talk about us with a sense of awe. I'd spent many a day locked in this here office, sittin' back tryin' to decide which college most deserved my considerable talents." It was obvious from the expression on his face that it remained a question that he was still struggling with thirty years later.

"Is that ethical?" I asked, trying to reel in the conversation that was beginning to drift away from Abe.

"Don't talk to me about ethical when those frickin' periodical schools do it all the time," as he spoke he looked as though he might come right over the desk at me.

"You mean parochial?"

He stared at me, clearly choosing to ignore my correction, but calming down slightly. "Like I said, they buy their teams while the public schools have to work with the frickin' leftovers. My God, we were gonna do something important — give kids a chance to play on a good team in high school. I mean, what do people talk about when they get old? They talk about what they did in high school," he seemed disappointed that I wasn't being caught up in the story and sharing his enthusiasm, as I'm sure his normal audience did down at Dino's. "All of my friends do, this whole town does. It would have been great," the frustration that his dreams had failed to materialize was still apparent in his eyes.

bertco2: A sad commentary. I wish that I had something more profound to offer.

pistevo: "The game, you were telling me about the game," I said as I found myself backing slightly away from his desk.

"Yeah, so I was, so I was. It's a battle, I mean a real war. Neither team could hold a lead. Four flagrant fouls called in the first half alone. Jimmy Foyton took four stitches in his chin within the first two minutes. They didn't even bother to wipe the blood off the ball in those days, ya just kept playin'. It got so rough that nobody for neither team was allowed to shoot in the paint without some serious pain bein' put on em'. Late in the fourth quarter we start gettin' in trouble. We're talkn' the kind of trouble I feared all along. They had a deep bench, playn' a ten-man rotation. Us, we're playn' six, signs of wear are beginning to show, and the fouls are pilin' up. I mean we'd just played a hard fought game against one of those Jewish — Catholic — frickin' — private type — cheatin' — schools the night before. With one minute to play, we're down by four with the ball, so I call our final time out to give em' one last blow. I says, 'get the ball to Abe, let's ride him home.' Mind you I never called him Shit-Head, no matter what anyone said, he was a fine young man back in those days," he pointed at me as he spoke.

"Anyways, we inbound the ball and Abe goes the length of the floor, splits the lane, and lays a high glasser over their 6'7" center," he was now playing the game out in his office. "Left him swattin' at nothing by empty space. We're down by two. Now, they try to take the air out of the ball," he laughed to himself. "If there's one thing I've learned in my years as a coach, it's that a runnin' team ain't no good at killin' the clock. Just not the way they're built to think. So we sit back, and when they pass it to their worst shooter, we hammer him. I mean this kid is a great boarder with arms thick as my legs, fact went on to play some D-1 pigskin if my memory does me right, but as for being a baller, a real bricklayer. The front end of the one and one hits nothing but air. The kid was so nervous I actually felt sorry for him. So now, it's our ball with forty-seconds left and Abe plays it like a song, just like I taught him ya know?" he glanced at me. "He beats a double team at half court, sizes up the defense, and pulls up for a nineteen foot jumper that sees nothing but the bottom of the net. Tie game. Now, it's their turn to call a time out."

"I'm just tellin' the boys to relax, sure their coach is tellin' them to keep the ball in their shooter's hands, wind the clock down, and take one last shot in regulation. They make it, it's game over and they're the champs. Miss, and with how tired our boys were and all of our foul trouble, they gotta feel good 'bout their chances in O.T. But their point guard is an excitable fifteen-year-old sophomore, and he sees brickman unguarded, so he tosses the rock down to him. As soon as the ball left his hands I heard their coach scream even above the roar of the crowd, but it was too late. We, of course, being well schooled in the intricacies of the game, mug the kid. Fifteen-seconds to go, tie game, and the kid hits the front end. I mean he banks the frickin' thing home from the line. If it hadn't been the State Finals I probably would have clapped for him myself. He's so relieved that he made the first one that he comes up four feet short on the second. I mean, it was so short that at first I thought he was tossin' the frickin' thing back to the ref," he stood shaking his head. "To this day I've never seen anyone miss a throw by that much, not even in a game with ten year old girls playin'."

"Anyways, there we were, down one, fifteen-seconds to go. Everyone in the building knows that Mr. First Team All-State two years in a row Abraham Lincoln is about to decide the game. One shot and he was destined to have everyone in these parts remember his name for generations to come. We inbound the ball off a high pick and he's bringin' it up. They double-team him once, twice, again, and then with four-seconds to go he's hammered just as he lets it fly. Abe is thrown to the floor as the ball kisses off the glass and falls through. But see, the ref has obviously never seen a game of hoops, and waves it off. Everybody's screaming. Our fans have flooded out onto the floor, but their coach is just standing there pointing to the ref who says it was before the shot. The P.A. announcer comes on and tells everyone to get back into their seats as the refs huddle at the center of the court to try to decide what to do. Bein' that the refs are all down state boys, I know what's comin'. After several minutes, they step out and give the signal for a one and one, no shot."

"Was it the right call?" I asked

"Hell's bells no. I've seen the tape a thousand times. Everybody round here has," he honestly seemed a bit put off that I hadn't seen the tape, hadn't everyone? "Not only was he in the act of shooting," he continued, "there was no contact until after the ball had left his hand."

"So they blew the call," I responded.

"They blew the call, big time. Never been a moment of doubt in the mind of anyone in these parts who's seen the tapes. And that would be everybody."

"So Abe actually had won the game, the State Championship," I said, half statement and half a question. "He was the hero for the second straight year."

"He did. No question about it," he clearly saw no conflict in his position.

"Then why all the anger if you know that he made *the* shot?"

"*The shot, the shot*, the ref waved off *the shot*," he spit as he spoke. "*The shot* never happened. *The throw* happened, and he didn't make *the throw*." I could tell that he wanted me to ask a question, but I just sat there staring at him, and after a few awkward seconds he continued. "The refs brought him back to the line down by one. I mean, what difference did it make? This was the leading scorer in the state at better than thirty-seven points per game. The captain of the All-State Team. The same kid that hit the winning shot in the State Championship the year before. He couldn't miss; bad call or not, it was our game to win and he was the best player in the gym. No, *the shot* didn't matter. Shouldn't have mattered," he turned away from me as he spoke. "First throw, bottom of the net. Tie game and I started straighten' my tie for the team picture. I mean, the year before I was so excited that I looked like frickin' John Madden on the front page of the Free Press. Then, it happened," he squared himself as if he were preparing for a free throw, then went through and completed the shooting motion. "He put the ball up soft as a feather, I mean the kid had a shooter's touch that was poetry in motion. When it left his hand I knew it was down, it was silk."

"But it wasn't," I replied.

"Damnedest thing I ever did see. Almost appeared that it hit the net so flush that it popped back out. Yeah, he missed," he shook his head as he spoke, still looking as if he was surprised that it didn't go in even after all these years.

"And the game slipped away in overtime just as you had feared."

"We were blown out ten to two. It was like we suddenly forgot how to play the game. I've never seen such a helpless group of puppies on the floor."

"Even Abe?"

"Abe, hells bells no, I sent him to the locker room after he missed *the* throw. I simply couldn't stand the sight of him wearing the school colors. At that moment he was no longer a part of my team, or for that matter, this here town. We played the O.T. without him. I was so absolutely and totally disgusted with him that I didn't even allow him back on the team bus for the ride back home after the game."

"You sent your All-State player to the dressing room before the overtime of the State Championship?" Why would you do that? From everything you've told me, he carried the team."

"He let down this city, can't you understand that?" It appeared to be a genuine question. "He took us straight down the crapper. It was ours, and he gave it away. It's not like we was asking Shaq to make *the* throw, we was asking Abraham Lincoln." It was obviously perfectly logical to him. "Once I explained my position to the boys down at Dino's, the entire town was on my side."

"But even you concede that if the refs would have called the game correctly he would have been the hero. In reality, he did the job, he hit *the* shot."

"Do you think anybody remembers that outside of this forgotten little town? Do you think knowing that helped me recruit ballers the next fall? Do you think that Judd Heathcoat called me over to his office the next morning to discuss my availability to take on the seat next to him on the

Spartan bench that fall? Does the Magic Man send me a birthday card every year? It's possible that he doesn't even remember that I named both my son and daughter after him even though I sent him announcements via certified mail. No sir, all history shows is that we lost that game, and if he would have made *the* throw, it would tell a much different story. This town would not have had to crawl back north with its tail between its legs filled with shame."

"Shame, you were the defending State Champs coming off a fifty-three game winning streak, it should have been one of the proudest times in this town's history."

He reached in the bottom of a drawer, and after a few seconds of rummaging, pulled out a yellowed newspaper article that had been ripped along the edges and placed it in front of me. "I'm probably the only person in town that still has a copy of this. Everyone else burned theirs years ago at the bonfire." It was a black and white picture of Abe putting up the winning shot from just out past the top of the key in the previous State Championship game.

bertco2: Would that be *a* bonfire, or *the* bonfire?

pistevo: I must have started to adapting to his way of thinking; I assumed it was *the* bonfire. The story was just moving ahead so quickly that I never inquired.

"The kid that hit that shot was a hero, an idol to all the young kids in this community. One missed throw and that very same community was shattered beyond repair," his tone instantly changed from quiet and distant to loud and in my face. "Do you realize we haven't won fifty-three games total since that frickin' day. This has to be one of the worst basketball programs in the entire state. Even our own parents don't bother to show up for the games. Most days I don't waste the time to practice. The only way I can get the kids to show up for games on time is to promise that the first five in the locker room get to start. That usually guarantees six kids will at least make an effort to get to the game. There have been years gettin' five kids to show was a problem. I've dressed kids as young as the seventh grade just to put a team on the floor. Our conference kicked our hoops team out years ago cause it just got too dang embarrassing."

"That kind of record would cost many coaches their job," I tried to phrase it as politely as possible.

"You gotta to be kiddin'; after the first State Championship I was given a life-time contract. Didn't realize that one year later it was going to become a prison sentence. There isn't a coach in the entire state that'd take this job. Do I need go on?"

"So then Abe went away to college." I realized he was going to go on indefinitely if I didn't keep his story moving along.

"Yeah, he went away, and good riddance. After that game I wouldn't have thought that he could sink any lower, but with offers from Michigan, Michigan State, Indiana — damn near every frickin' D-1 program in this time zone — he proved that he wasn't done lettin' us down. The only class D player in years to get that kind of national attention. He could have opened up recruiting to small town kids all across the U.P., but no, the bonehead didn't have the smarts to go to any of them. The chance to play on the tube every weekend, the big dance in March, the opportunity to start redeemin' himself in the eyes of this here school, but he was a lost cause by then. He threw his whole future away and blew them all off," somehow, in the course of a single statement he went from mad to depressed to frustrated to despondent, then started the cycle again.

"Where did he go?"

"Harvard! Can you imagine that? A basketball player who thinks his future is in Connecticut."

"Harvard is in Boston," it took me a few seconds to gather my thoughts and try to follow him.

"So what's your point?"

"Boston is in Massachusetts."

"Whatever, like that makes any real difference. I mean the kid was a basketball player. I didn't even know Harvard had a frickin' basketball team. I can honestly tell you that to this very day I've never seen them play on the tube. Not even on ESPN II where they're so desperate I've been forced to watch women's racquetball for an entire evening. I mean, I don't even know what their colors are. Honestly, I doubt he ever really played out there. I heard some say that he was All-Conference all four years or some nonsense, but really, what kinda conference can a school like that even be in? To this day I can't imagine what that kid was thinkin' going to a place like that. What kinda future could a school like Harvard offer a talented young baller?"

My list of questions was growing, however, at the same time, I sensed that it was time to draw this chapter of Abe's story to a conclusion before Coach Reed completely broke down. How could anyone be so out of touch, so shallow, or for lack of a better explanation, so stupid?   It was appalling, but I realized that my deteriorating attitude might result in closing the door on any future conversations with him if I kept pushing. All I could think of was to politely excuse myself and quickly slip out, claiming that I had another pressing appointment.

He stood up and turned his back toward me as he stared out the window, obviously, emotionally exhausted. "Probably just as well, Doc says it's not good for me to talk 'bout it. Says my blood pressure shoots to the moon and is gonna send me to an early grave. I mean, for the love of God, the fruitcake wants me to start going to yoga classes to learn how to control my emotions. Can you picture me in tights doin' yoga?" I tried not to.

I was looking down at my notepad, reading, but not seeing anything. Abe seemed nearly perfect. He had been the player of a lifetime for any small town, and managed to accomplish it all while maintaining an academic level that landed him at Harvard. Now, all they remembered was one shot, err, throw. And after only an hour poking around, I had complete confidence that if the idiot coach would have just left Abe in the game, he would have scored the winning basket again, and they would both be legendary in these parts.

bertco2: And Abe would probably still be stuck in that town retelling the story of his winning shot down at Dino's every night after dropping out of college to go back home and bask in his glory days.

pistevo: Perhaps you're right, maybe the guy, or for that matter the entire community, did him a favor.

bertco2 Unfortunately, little would have changed for Coach Reed. With his personality, he was destined to create a permanent state of personal crisis around him. Michigan State wasn't going to call, and he likely would have focused his embitterment toward them instead of Abe.

pistevo: Dragging the boys at Dino's down with him. Although, for nearly everyone else, that would have been the better alternative.

bertco2: Precisely, they were simply waiting for a leader that would provide them with an excuse to underachieve and complain.

"I appreciate all the insight," I said as I folded up my notebook and stood. "If I have any other questions, I'll come back and see you," I extended my hand.

He turned back around looking much calmer. "Always glad to be of help to the authorities. If you want any help reviewing your report, stop on back and I'd be happy to check it for accuracy. I got the whole story locked up right here," he said as he tapped his temple again. "Ya know, I minored in English back when I was playin' football, so I could make sure it reads good."

"I appreciate the offer," I said, and then quickly stepped out of his office and carefully pulled the door closed.

Standing in the hallway trying to take in everything Coach Reed had said, I suddenly felt compelled to walk down the hall to the gym and take a look around. It was much smaller than where I went to school, but probably not much different from thousands of other gymnasiums scattered across the country. What struck me as I gazed around was that I normally would have expected to see a State Championship banner proudly displayed from the rafters along side the other tattered conference championships and various awards that the local teams had accumulated throughout the years. Indeed, there were banners from other sports and years, but nothing that related to the time Abe had ruled the gym. Under the scoreboard was a wooden board that carefully detailed all the school records in various sports, including the scoring record for basketball for a single game of thirty-five set by someone named Roman in 1986. This, despite Abe's thirty-seven points per game average his senior year.

His time in that gym had to have been the most memorable in the school's history. I could almost imagine the capacity crowds, noise too loud to speak to the person next to you, the smell of popcorn, as the Knights reigned as a powerhouse in these walls. A town that few had ever heard of, and fewer yet ever seen, had carved out an identity. It's a wonderful time when players are local heroes and role models to the younger kids, parents analyze and replay the highlights of the night as others congratulate them on the outcome of the game. In good and bad ways, it's an experience unique to small town America. I can recall sitting in the stands of football and basketball games when I was ten years old watching some of our hometown games. They remain some of the most vivid memories of my youth. Now, it was as if that piece of history had been erased from time. It wasn't just Abe who had lost those memories, it was the entire community. I left the gym depressed, still thinking about my own youth, when suddenly someone stepped in front of me.

"Ya know, anyone who hangs with Shit-Head must be a shit-head himself."

It was the young girl from the office. It wasn't so much what she said as how she said it — with complete and utter contempt. I couldn't even respond. I just nodded in her direction and continued walking. Have you ever heard of such a bizarre reaction?

bertco2:   I can only hope that if I have kids of my own someday, they grow up to perform as poorly as your client. It sounds like the entire school might benefit from paying me a visit. With the amount of time that I expect needs to be invested, I could probably work out some kind of group rate.

pistevo: I have to go. I'm sitting down in the lobby and it appears that I'm wearing out my welcome on this line. We can meet up tomorrow night and see what I've learned during the day, if anything. If you aren't around, I'll just drop it in your box. Until then, could it get any stranger???

bertco2:   I can hardly wait.

DAY SIX

THE LINCOLN FAMILY

SEPTEMBER 13TH

7:17 p.m.

pistevo: Glad to see that you could make it.

bertco2:   I managed to squeeze you into my schedule. Admittedly, it was quite a challenge. Hopefully, you have gained some knowledge worthy of my significant personal sacrifice.

pistevo: I was just looking through my notes, and this is going to be a long one, so you may want to get something to drink and sit back and relax.

bertco2:   Already brewed a pot of fully caffeinated coffee. Other than a few obligatory bathroom breaks, I should be wide awake for the duration. It has to be more interesting than the cases I listened to today where the correct diagnosis would have been, 'get over it.'

pistevo: I traveled to the outskirts of town this morning to meet some of Abe's extended family. Quite a unique group I must say. Although, at this point, anything less would have been a bit of a disappointment. They live in a modular ranch that's only a few years old that Abe bought for his mother shortly after the infomercials went national. After expecting the worst, it really was a very comfortable home. His mother told me SH was the perfect son, helped to carry the family through the dark years after her husband passed on, and pays most of the bills to this day.

bertco2:   She called him SH?

pistevo: Much of the time. Occasionally, she referred to him as Abe.

Let me start with his father. Philip Lincoln was born and raised in the area, and eventually returned after an eight year stint in the army which included two years in Korea. He came home, married Abe's mom, and from what I can tell, spent the next twenty-five years sitting in front of the TV drinking beer and pouring through piles of books that his wife would bring home from the library.

bertco2:   An interesting contrast.

pistevo: From the lone remaining picture of him on the wall, he was a rather handsome, proper looking military man at the time of their marriage. There were conspicuously no later photos of the man that he would become. The description his wife painted of their married years was of a crude, overweight man, who was routinely intoxicated and never managed to work a single day their entire marriage. Still, in a rather sad way, I had to admire her because she refused to openly criticize him, referring to him only as a man who had led a troubled life. The events of the war weighed heavily on his mind, so she said. It was difficult to draw any meaningful information out of her that would have painted an accurate picture of him. Repeatedly, she claimed that she misses him each and every night even to this day.

He lost his driver's license in 1973 following a third drunk driving offense and never left the yard again, save his nightly walks to the party store a quarter mile down the road, until his death in June of 1986. He choked to death on his own vomit on the back porch after a four day drinking binge. Abe's sister Carol found him upon arriving home from school one afternoon. A tragic life by all appearances. I'm afraid there is little else to say about him right now.

His mom reminisces about raising Abe like it was part of the Cleaver family. A great kid, always helping around the house, and eager to learn. It was obvious that she was proud of him as she beamed throughout the conversation. I thought it was interesting that she talked about him for nearly an hour and never mentioned anything related to basketball, which until that conversation had been the only reference point that I had encountered since arriving. All of her memories are simply of her son, the kind of person he was growing up, and the man that he is now.

Ten years younger, his sister Carol still lives at home. She moved out at eighteen, then found her way home in 1993 after less than a year of an abusive marriage. From what I can tell, she's pretty much a lost cause. Unable to hold down a job, she's at the bar every afternoon by three, and most nights closes the place down. A beautiful girl in her youth, she has aged very poorly by all accounts. Looking at pictures around the house, I would have guessed her a lot closer to fifty than approaching forty. I haven't had a chance to talk to her, but I plan on doing that before I leave town. At least I know where to find her.

A real twist comes in with her son. Raised on gifts from his uncle, with a father who was never mentioned, and a drunk for a mother, the deck was obviously stacked against him. To make matters worse, he is the spitting image of his Uncle Abe. At fifteen he is a solid 6'1" and 175 pounds, and is the starting quarterback on the varsity football team. The kid, Kennedy, is nearly perfect.

bertco2:   Wait, Kennedy, as in JFK?

pistevo: The same.

bertco2:   And the fixation with historical figures in the family lives on.

pistevo: His mother has a big picture of him over the bed. It seems she was born on the anniversary of the JFK assassination. As a child she grew up with a picture of Jesus in between Lincoln and Kennedy hanging in her room. Kennedy has the same three pictures hanging above his headboard. Ma Lincoln believes that they are the two greatest men short of Christ who ever walked the earth.

bertco2:   So every morning, the kid wakes up staring at two presidents that were assassinated. What a cheerful way to start the day.

pistevo: True, but like I said, this kid is almost too good to be true. A straight A student, he holds down an evening job, is active in church, has movie star looks and is THE star athlete. In his spare time he is raising his eleven year old sister who came into the picture with no explanation from anyone. I kept hearing about Kennedy in conversations around town as I tried to garnish the school's athletic legacy, but was caught with my mouth hanging open when I was introduced to him up at grandma's house.

He gets up every night when mom stumbles home and cleans her up for bed. In the morning, he gets sis off to school after feeding her, and then heads out to school himself. At lunch he comes home, gets his mother up, and tries to get some food into her. At night, it's practice, dinner, stories with his sister, then off to his room to study for several hours. He talks about all of this like every other kid in the world bears the same burden at fifteen.

I may write more on Kennedy a little later, but there is at least one more thing worthy of mention before I move on. As I was talking to him, he sat on the edge of the couch fidgeting with a football helmet that had the initials SF taped on the front. When I stood to leave I asked him what the initials stood for. He informed me that all the players had their equipment labeled so that it didn't get mixed up. He claimed that

SF was a strange name that he had picked up somewhere as a child — Shit-Face.

bertco2: They appear to be a family of extremes, albeit extremes with a frighteningly negative consistency. So, what are your plans for tomorrow?

pistevo: I'm still working through that. I want to give a thorough read of all of my notes before considering what's next.

bertco2: Probably as good a plan as any. I have a late appointment tomorrow; how about trying to meet up closer to 6:00?

pistevo: Sounds good, I don't have any real schedule anyway.

Bertco2: Talk to you then.

DAY SEVEN

UNCLE LEWIS

SEPTEMBER 14TH

5:57 p.m.

bertco2:   Productive day?

pistevo: None of my conversations today were particularly meaningful; however, I have to tell you about Uncle Lewis. He lives down the road from his sister in a run down shack that somehow manages to lean in multiple directions. Among the garbage strewn about, every car he has ever driven is rusting in the yard. The grass, or more precisely weeds, haven't been cut in years, making it appear abandoned, or more honestly, begging to be condemned. Lewis doesn't have a phone, so Ma Lincoln, as she is called, ran me over in her brand new extended cab Ford 150 pickup that Abe had delivered to her last month as a birthday present. Ma described Uncle Lewis as trouble since the day he was born. A drunk by the time he was fifteen, he was thrown out of school for punching a teacher that failed him in a class, leaving him ineligible for the track team.

bertco2:   Probably safe to assume he carried some of the family athletic genes.

pistevo: A good assumption, but we'll never know for certain. According to Ma, the the coach of the team he was so upset about being ineligible for, didn't even realize he was on the team because he hadn't attended a single meet or practice the entire season.

bertco2:   Apparently, discipline and decision-making were never strengths of his.

pistevo: Apparently not. Ma went on to tell me that by his late teens Lewis was a frequent bar brawler, and tended to spend more nights in the county jail than at home. Finally, he was hit in the face with a tire iron that cost him his front teeth and right eye. After that, he retreated to their dad's deserted hunting cabin only to leave for food, smokes and beer. Which from all appearances, are the limitations on his world.

"Lewis, it's Ma," she screamed at the house as she climbed out of the truck. "He always sleeps with that blasted shotgun, and it's best to make certain you don't catch him unawares." At this point I was beginning to have second thoughts concerning the wisdom of my visit.

Ma hammered on the door, paused for a moment, then let herself in, banging loudly to make certain that he had heard her. Uncle Lewis sat in the corner of the one-room shack on a badly sagging bed. He was propped up against the wall with the stub of a hand rolled cigarette dangling from his mouth, his right hand on a double barrel shotgun, his left clutching a TV remote control. Some game show I had never seen was on, and as we entered he motioned for us to be quiet without looking up. There was a collective sigh from the audience, and he clicked off the TV shaking his head.

"Dumb arse," he flicked his lit cigarette butt toward the set where it fell among the scatted remains of several dozen like butts. "Somebody ought to screen these shows for dumb arses before they parade them out there for the world to see. Every day it's the same thing all day long," he shook his head as he spoke, still not looking at either one of us. "Never would've guessed there were so many dumb arses in the world, but they just keep bringin' em' in," he reached over and grabbed a bottle of what appeared to be homemade wine off of the night stand and took a long drink. "Some place they got a factory spewing 'em out day and night. Apparently, they're working a lot of O.T.," he paused and carefully eyed me for the first time. "Now, what brings the uptown folks down here to the slum?" It was obvious that there was more than a little tension between the two of them.

"This fellow here wanted to ask you a few questions," Ma Lewis said.

I stood waiting for her to continue, but instead was greeted by the sound of the door slamming behind her. I whirled around to try to persuade her to stay, but it was too late, she was gone. I turned back to Lewis as he was taking another long drink, examining me in a manner that left me feeling very much like the intruder that I suddenly realized I was.

"So boy, what's on your mind?" It was hard not to stare at his bad eye, which was completely white, and seemed to be permanently fixed on me regardless of what direction he was looking.

"I just wanted to talk to you for a minute about your nephew Abe, it seems that he has quite a reputation in these parts." It occurred to me that I might want to ask my questions in a manner that discouraged any lengthy discussion.

He looked at me for a moment, lit a fresh cigarette off of a stick he pulled from the wood stove, and then took a long drag as he looked away. "You might as well know right off that I don't care none 'bout basketball. Never did, never will. They say he was good, but never even saw the boy play. If you want to talk 'bout that, you've come a long way for nothin'," he talked through a cloud of smoke.

I paused to ensure he was done. "So where did he pick up the name Shit-Head?" Thirty-seconds into my interrogation I already knew that I wanted to get straight to the point of my visit and get out of there as quickly as possible.

He was still sizing me up when he finally spoke. "When he was about three years old he was walkin' across a pasture and slipped in some cow manure. When he stood up he had it all matted in his hair. The way I see it, the name just stuck in much the same way as the crap," he somehow managed a drink with his cigarette still dangling from the corner of his mouth.

"That's it, he slipped in some cow manure?"

"That's it," he leaned slightly forward. "Why are people always looking for the complicated answer to life's simple questions? If folks would have just looked at his dang hair the answer was matted right there."

There was a brief silence as we stared at each other. "What about Kennedy and the name Shit-Face?" I seemed to be following a fairly narrow line of questioning.

"Who?"

"Kennedy, Carol's boy."

"Never met him. Didn't even know she had kid. A real arse no doubt."

"Honestly, he's quite an exceptional kid."

"Really, go figure," he paused for another drink, carefully watching me. "Shit-Face, huh? My guess, unlike his uncle who fell backward, he fell forward."

"Excuse me."

"Shit-Face, the name, he probably fell face down," he took another drink. "Why look any farther than Abe's answer? Like I said, folks try to make things much harder than they are."

"Okay, yeah, perhaps," I was right on my toes with the articulate replies.

We both were silent for a few seconds. "You done?"

"Yeah, I guess that should do it," another snappy, well thought out reply.

"Now, my next show's 'bout to come on, so either sit down, shut up and grab a drink quick like, or hit the door. When Vanna's on, ain't nobody gonna distract me," he smiled slightly. "Unless you have another witty question for me," he looked away, clearly signaling that the conversation, and his patience with my intrusion, were over.

"Thanks, I'll be going," and with that I stepped out as rapidly as possible.

Clearly, when you have lost an intellectual battle with a man that never finished high school, rarely leaves his house, and views that world through game shows, it's time to retreat. Standing on the porch, just to the left I noticed a pile of about a half dozen TV sets that appeared to have been blown apart by a shotgun. A soft rain had started to fall, but I wanted to put as much space as possible between myself and

Lewis, so I pulled up my collar and headed back toward the hotel, for the first time realizing that when Ma Lincoln bailed on me, so had my ride. An hour later, after walking down dirt roads through what had developed into a soft rolling thunderstorm, I was safely back in my room, and emotionally ready to pack up and go home with Abe's situation completely unresolved. It seems that my five star education left out a few things — like apparently everything.

bertco2: Sounds like you had another full day. When do you want to meet up again? I'd like to go through my notes and give all of this some thought.

pistevo: How about the same time tomorrow night. That extra hour works better for me. After I get some sleep I'll be ready to go back out and do some more sleuthing. Right now, I just want a hot shower and a cold beer.

bertco2: Talk to you then.

DR. COCHRAN

Dr. Cochran rose from the chair behind her desk, watching the last few students of her final class for the afternoon straggle out. Same class, same lecture, same responses from the students as every semester. Still, it was a living, and it beat the steady stream of upper-class clients with problems that were typically more perception than reality that she had dealt with during her several years in private practice.

At moments like these, when she thought back on all of her years in graduate school and felt as though she was underachieving, her thoughts turned to the twins. Now that they were in school, the job at the college gave her the flexibility to make sure that she could be there with them when they returned home on Monday, Wednesday and Friday. Her husband had been able to rework his schedule so that he could greet them from the bus on Tuesday and Thursday. Not exactly the family life she had imagined years earlier, but it seemed to fit their needs at the moment, and increasingly, appeared more sane than any of her friends. Still, she yearned for something to inject a little variety into life.

She grabbed her briefcase, banged on the door of a colleague who was trying to start a class of his own, then headed out to her car for the half hour commute home. The twins would be off to soccer practice with their dad later that evening, and the package that she had received following her conversation last night with Steven had left her eager to get home and read through the notes one more time.

They had been members of several psychology chat groups, and their mutual interest in bizarre cases kept them popping up in the same places on the Internet. When he forwarded the information on his friend's case, she had been flattered that he had included her and quickly read through the pages before turning in. Throughout the next day, even as she worked, it managed to keep creeping into her thoughts, and she found herself starting some notes of her own. Maybe she missed the clinical aspects of the profession more than she realized, or possibly this case was just more intriguing than most. An evening online with an old friend, although she had never met him, a potential new acquaintance, a case that was strange even in the world of psychological analysis, a glass of wine and a quiet house. It was shaping up to be a good evening.

DAY EIGHT

DOC

SEPTEMBER 15TH

6:03 p.m.

pistevo: I had an interesting day to tell you about if you're out there somewhere. This may make for an intriguing conversation, even when considering the last couple of days.

bertco2:   Here and waiting.   I have been very busy working some on my associates since last night. I hope you don't mind, but I invited a few of my cohorts to join in on the conversation.   I've already copied over our files to date. They will probably pop you some mail sometime in the near future.

Two. The first is David Marriott, he works with me here at the office. A few years my senior, he was my mentor when I first came on board. He won't be able to join us until our next session, but I think that he will be a valuable addition. The second is Dr. Lisa Cochran. She practiced clinical psychology for a few years after getting her Ph.D., then settled here in Rochester as the Director of Psychology at a local junior college. Turns out that she lives less than a mile away from me, but like you, I met her here in a chat room. Doc is online with us right now.

imdoc: I really appreciate being included. This is a fascinating case you're pursuing. Although, you might be surprised how unusual it isn't. I detested my time spent in counseling — too much complaining. However, after teaching day after day in front of disinterested, underachieving eighteen year olds, a bit of dabbling in pop psychology may prove therapeutic.

pistevo: Glad to have you aboard Dr. Cochran. It's become fairly obvious over the past couple of days that I need all the advice I can get on this case. Every day brings further evidence that I truly understand very little about human nature.

imdoc: Please call me either Lisa or Doc. I use so little of the overpriced formal education I pursued so diligently that I have grown uncomfortable with the formal distinction.

CAROL

6:09 p.m.

bertco2:   Last time we 'talked' you were hoping to get a chance to sit down with your client's sister. Any luck?

pistevo: I spent some quality time with her earlier today. I would describe it as bizarre, but I've used that term so many times since I arrived here that I fear I've minimized its effectiveness at best, or more likely, completely bastardized it. Allow me to try to recreate the scene.

The setting: The Wilderness Tavern. A small wooden structure downtown that was built around the time of the Great Depression, which incidentally, was the last time that it appears it was cleaned. I was advised that it was the only location I would find her sobriety at a level suitable for any type of conversation; however, I needed to get there early in the afternoon.

bertco2:   A peculiar combination of location and optimal mental alertness.

pistevo: Indeed. True to form, the bar is located on the main street in an old wooden structure that is leaning a bit to the North, (as is the entire block). When I first walked in I thought that the place was deserted because it was so dark, but after a few moments, my eyes began to adjust, and I could make out the subtle movements of a few patrons slouched over their tables. The smell of stale beer, smoke and greasy food made my nostrils flare as the door swung shut behind me. Carol, or I assumed as much because there were no other women in the place, sat at the very end of the bar at the farthest possible point from the door. She was leaning against the wall, slowly stirring her drink and reading from some type of thick book. She was using the light from a Budweiser display sign to read by. I crossed the bar, my shoes slightly sticking to the floor, and slid up on the stool next to her.

"What do you want?" A gruff voice came from behind me that was so loud I jumped.

"Nothing, I was just hoping to have a few words with Carol."

"Then you and your scrawny arse should hit the door. This here's a bar. We serve drink, food and more drink. If you don't want none, you're in the wrong place and costn' me money by takin' up a seat a payin' customer could use." (There were only five customers in the place including myself). "Besides, Carol here is my girl and I don't take to strangers hittin' on her, lest they're buyin' her food and drink. In that case it suits me fine cause she costs me more than I can afford most days."

I sat on my stool trying to decide where to start, fascinated that Carol's eyes had never shown any acknowledgment of our conversation taking place only a few feet from her seat, or for that matter, my arrival in general.

bertco2:   A typical response you get from women?

pistevo: Regrettably, all too typical.

Turning my attention back to the bartender, "I guess I'll just have a coke."

"A coke, you come to my bar and order a coke. That'll be twice the price of a rum and coke just for drinkin' like a little girl."

"And a Jack Daniel's," Carol never looked up. "As long as he's buying drinks," her voice was clear and firm.

"A coke and Jack Daniel's, all right," he said as he turned and went to the far end of the bar.

"So what do you want?" She thumped her book closed and turned toward me, looking me straight in the eye.

"I've been talking to a few people about your brother Abe," I was going to say more, but she cut me short.

"How is the ole' boy? You know, I really miss having him around. He was the one person in this town that I could sit down and have a reasonable discussion with. There are precious few around here I truly enjoy talking to as much as I did my big bro," her face lit as she spoke.

I stared at her for a moment in surprise, even though I knew that at this point in my journey nothing should surprise me. "He's doing well. Good career, lovely wife, new baby. He's doing well. I'm sure that you would be proud of him."

"I always knew that he would. I know that he talks regularly with Ma, and he still makes an effort to stay in touch with me," she paused and her voice softened, "but I really think that it's best if he keeps his distance from both me and this place." We stared at each other for several seconds. "Well, you came all the way from who knows where to ask me about my brother, but now that you're here, you suddenly seem to have little to say."

"If you don't mind, before talking about Abe I would like to ask you a few things about yourself."

The bartender slammed the drinks down in front of us along with two large bowls of what appeared to be vegetable soup. "I decided that the two of you looked hungry so I added a couple of bowls to your tab." Carol winked at him and slugged down half of the Jack Daniel's that he had brought to her in a drinking glass. "

You'll be thankin' me for it."

"Thanks." It looked more like gruel and soup, but I must admit, smelled quite good.

He stood leering over us with this stupid grin on his face that left me a bit disconcerted until I took a drink of my coke and found it to be heavily laden with whiskey. I put the glass down

as I hacked quietly and turned toward the bartender who was now wearing a smile from ear to ear having received the reaction from me that he was hoping for.
"No charge," he said, and turned on his heels and headed down the bar and into the back room.

"That's his favorite gag. He does it to everyone who comes in here and orders a coke," she picked up her soupspoon as she spoke. "Unfortunately, he also does it to some of the regulars. He thinks they're too stupid to catch on. What they're doing is getting a whiskey for the price of a coke. Which despite all of his bravado for charging you double, I've never known him to remember to charge the premium, and if he did, there are few in these parts that would pay it. Joe isn't exactly the sharpest stick you'll run across."

I was tempted to ask if she was really 'his girl', and if so, why, if she recognized his obvious limitations. She glanced up at me as if she was reading my mind, or, more likely, had thought about it many times.

"He's a good man, if not, shall we say, particularly clever. I have learned that good is much more difficult to find, and far more valuable."

"And so you remain his gal,"

She rolled her shoulders. "In manner of speaking. It seems to be important that he can refer to me as such. In reality," she motioned around the bar, "this is the only place you will ever find us together. We've actually never been on anything that even remotely resembled a real date. And yet," she said as she lifted her drink.

"It works for you?" I replied.

"It fits what I need in my life. At least for now," she smiled slightly. "Realistically, for the remainder of my days. We have an — I drink — he provides drinks — I sit by him — he sits by me, common law marriage. Pretty much right out of a Disney tale don't you think?"

"And so you come in here and sit day after day."

"So it would appear," she took another drink.

I was growing depressed at the conversation. "Do you mind if I ask what you are reading?"

"It's a Portuguese literature compilation. I tend to read things like this in a variety of languages to keep my mind sharp," she smiled. "Even in this place I'm allowed to pretend. Hopefully, its effects will help to counter this," she picked up her drink. "You look surprised," it was obvious that my response was amusing her.

I considered her for a moment, and then decided to be frank. "Honestly, I am. I was expecting something less of you."

"Ahh yes, promiscuous and a drunk. Getting a sordid reputation is not a difficult thing in a place such as this. Not that I have considered it worthy of making much of an effort to alter it."

"Do you blame any of this on Abe? I mean, that seems to be a common theme in these parts."

She stared at me over the top of her glass. "That's ridiculous. The people here all blame their sad existence on a botched free throw. I tend to blame my problems on a community that finds such inconsequential events as defining moments in time," she took another drink. "We're both wrong of course, we're simply all too weak and fearful to face life, and it's just far easier to find someone or something else to blame. That way, we don't have to do anything to get beyond our sorry states. My excuse is just more eloquent. A bit excessively philosophical, but," she shrugged her shoulders and returned to her soup.

"So you sit here all day drinking whiskey and reading foreign literature."

"Other times I write — even here everyone needs a hobby."

"What kind of writing?"

"It started out as thoughts and observations as I reflected on my experiences, but then took on a life of its own. A couple of months after I started, I had penned over five hundred pages. That was eight years ago, and I have written steadily since. Seventeen books in all. Romance, thrillers, literature, whatever came upon me at the time. Well over two million words now. My most recent challenge has been to take on the task of trying to combine them all into a single continuous volume that is intertwined with Tolkien's trilogy. I want to make sure that all the subtle details cut out of the Hollywood version get their just emphasis," she shrugged her shoulders again. "The bizarre meets popular culture. That is if fantasy can be considered pop. The kind of challenge that seems logical when these walls are your primary residence, and Jack Daniel's your closest friend.

The way that I look at it, my calendar is now filled for the remainder of my days."

"Have you ever tried to publish any this?"

"No, it's just for the pleasure of it. As I said, it fills the time; takes up the space so to speak. Besides, writers are only truly recognized posthumously if they honestly have anything of significance to offer. At least that's what my eighth grade English teacher told me, and she turned out to be such a fine example of leadership that she might have been right. Another consideration is that she never got around to reading anything by anyone still living."

"You sound a bit sarcastic."

"In truth, no. Even as an adult I have to reflect back that she was nearly perfect."

"And you're trying to drink yourself into immortality as quickly as possible so that you can grab the brass ring."

"Is that a question?"

"More of an observation."

"Perhaps," she said as she emptied her glass. "For better or worse, I have learned to accept what and who I am."
"Did you ever consider that you could be more?"

"Once upon a time in a far away land, perhaps I could have, but not now."

"And of your children?"

For the first time I saw a hint of pain in her eyes. She reached into her pocket and pulled out a swisher sweet, and striking a match, took a long, deep drag. She was obviously going to take her time and choose her words carefully.

"What's the objective?"

"The objective to what?"

"Raising kids,"

She caught me unprepared. The weakness that flashed across her face a moment before was now gone, and she had once again assumed complete control of our conversation.

"I guess that would be to raise happy, well adjusted kids that can take care of themselves and be contributing adults," she managed to keep

me off balance — it's not the kind of single sentence, all-encompassing definition, one has prepared for just such an occasion.
"And what did you find?" I sat silently staring at her. "Good kids, wouldn't you say? Some might even say exceptional," she said as she exhaled a cloud of smoke.

"Amazing kids." I thought it best not to try and elaborate.

"Go figure. Turning out so good I'm afraid to go home for fear I'll screw everything up."

"Do you believe that?" I could sense she was copping out on me.

A hint of a smile creased the corners of her mouth. "No, no, I do not believe that. Although, at the same time, they are turning out quite well in spite of my behavior, and I am still trying in my own rather pathetic way. Every day Kennedy and I sit together in the bathroom after about my fifth cup of coffee, and we talk. We talk about life, what's important, and what's not. Somehow, he has the capacity to look beyond what I am and hear the words. It's a wonderful talent that few can claim," she smiled as she spoke. "We talk about his goals, objectives, philosophies, whatever is on his mind. I tell him what I have absorbed from my readings throughout the night, he tells me about school, his friends, sports, and his feelings about God and life in general. And always, we speak of me, the choices I have made, and the obvious consequences which I must suffer through. The rest, for better or worse, I leave to my mother," she paused. "Yes, I know it's wrong, unfair and irresponsible, but the results, not the methods, are what really matter in the end. At least I have been able to persuade myself of that to a sufficient degree."

"And that's enough?"

Her tone became colder, "I am an alcoholic, and an actively practicing one. Of that I am not proud, but I am. I have great faith in mother, even though I fully recognize that I am being less than fair to her. She's the best, she likes to do it, and the kids are coping well."

"You say that regardless of the struggles you continue to deal with in your life?"

"Am I to hold her responsible for my weaknesses? I know I ask too much of her, but I harbor no illusions about who is to blame for the fact that I find myself wasting away in this seat day after day. I am," she raised her arms and motioned to the bar around her, "my own creation. I made many very bad choices early in life. They were bad and they were lasting. In the Biblical sense, I built my foundation on the sand, or more precisely, quick sand in my case."

"And your daughter?"

"Ahh yes, my daughter. She's a great kid and I wish that I was a better example to her, but alas, she is not my daughter," she clearly enjoyed the look of surprise in my eyes. "It's assumed as such, with my reputation and all, but much too convenient when one considers that I haven't been pregnant since Kennedy. What most people don't realize is that I probably have been 'intimate'," she made quote signs with her fingers, "less than anyone in this town." She took one last drag and crushed out her smoke, holding up her empty glass at the same time. Joe appeared from nowhere, poured more whiskey, and then silently slipped back out of sight.

"Then where did she come from?" my voice failed to disguise my intrigue.

"There was a young girl here in town who was with child, as they say. A few weeks after the delivery, she decided she wasn't ready to be a mother, so Ma took her in to try to get her over the hump."

"And the mother never returned after the baby was born."

"Not to stay, but I doubt Ma really ever encouraged her too. Hopefully, it has worked out best for everyone. She certainly is turning out to be a good kid. I haven't seen the mother around town in several years, so I assume that she has moved on. Not that my social calendar permits me to stay in close touch with the community."

"And Kennedy is taking to her like a sister."

She looked up. "He's wonderful to her. He couldn't care more for her if she was his own flesh and blood," she took a long drink. "Now, you wanted to ask about my brother," her tone suddenly changed indicating that she was growing uncomfortable, or tired, with the path our conversation had taken.

"Perhaps another time."

"Perhaps."

I slid down off of the stool. "I enjoyed our little talk, you are much more than you give yourself credit for." I could see a hint of appreciation in her eyes. "Listen," I pulled out my low budget business cards from my wallet. "I would like to see your writing. When you feel the mood, shoot me a copy, even if it's just in rough draft form. I'm a bit of a voracious reader who is always in search of something different."

She smiled politely as I handed her my card. We both knew that she probably would never share her work with anyone. Then, I turned my back on one of the most intriguing people I had ever met, and left the bar.

bertco2: I have to admit, that like you, I had formed a preconception toward the woman that is a bit different from what you encountered.

imdoc: Any mention of a formal education that led to her literary interests?

pistevo: I don't think so, although I never inquired about her directly. From what I can tell, she has rarely ventured beyond the edges of this obscure town.

imdoc: An interesting case — if we can call it that. I would enjoy turning over an abridged version to one of my first year classes to analyze as a group project. It would be fascinating to see what percentage of class failed to detect any abnormalities in the family.

pistevo: They probably would be as good at developing a meaningful conclusion as I am.

bertco2:   As much as I find his sister interesting and would like to help her deal with her demons, does what you learned talking to her tell us anything useful about Abe?

imdoc: Honestly, I believe that it does provide some insight. Even from the brief snapshots Steven has be able to provide us, Abe's family appears to be full of individuals of great promise and ability.   He has shown considerable academic and athletic abilities, his sister may be some kind of creative genius for all we know, and his nephew sounds like he has some gifts of his own. I would suggest that you do a little more digging around.   You may be surprised what you learn about his mother and father. Additionally, based on his dad's reading habits that Ma commented on, it might be interesting to stop by the local bookstore or library to see what they can offer. There has to be more to it than two family members who both like to get to intoxicated and then pour themselves into literature.   Lastly, a few minutes at football practice watching Kennedy interact with his team could prove insightful.

bertco2:   Great, when should we meet again?

pistevo: How about forty-eight hours? That will give me an opportunity to do a few last visits. After that, I'll need to start heading home. It will be a farewell gathering of sorts. Please keep in mind that when I leave here I need to have something meaningful to tell Abe if I'm going to feel good about my bill.

bertco2: Not that you aren't going to bill him regardless.

pistevo: Of course, just a matter of how I feel about it.

bertco2: You'll learn to get over that in the due course of time; the checks all cash the same.

imdoc: Any objections if I share some of this story with others?

pistevo: Anyone that you think might make a contribution is more than welcome. A group of your students might be exactly the perspective that's needed. We may get some interesting insight from an unexpected source.

bertco2: Until then.

DAVID

The office had cleared out early, which was the normal course of business during sunny summer afternoons. Not only were his fellow counselors eager to bail out and enjoy the weather during what had been a cold, rainy summer, even their clients that were desperately in need of help had started calling in early to reschedule, preferring to put their struggles off for a less pleasant day. David was always the last to leave — it had been that way since he founded the center nearly twenty years ago. It was ingrained in his psyche that being in charge automatically translated into unlocking the door in the morning, and locking it in the evening. It was part of the routine, and since his wife worked second shift at the hospital and their daughter was off to college, he had no real reason to hurry home anyway.

He grabbed the file that he had worked through with Robert that morning when both of their nine o'clock appointments failed to show, finding the story more intriguing than he had let on at the time. Robert had been after him for several days to participate in an online case that he was offering help on, but David had tried to maintain his distance and not become involved in his young associate's after-hours project. His experience had always taught him to keep work and friendships separated. This case, however, was almost more than he could walk away from. Robert had printed off the transcripts of the case from the first day and gone over them line by line with David, including all of his notes and thoughts from his own file. It had taken a full hour to get through all the details, but at least David could take some pride in the fact that Robert had followed his teaching on taking copious notes. As he constantly reinforced, you just never know where the key piece of information might be lurking that helps to unlock the real issues with a patient.

He stared at his computer screen for a few seconds. They would all be online at six, and he could jump into the middle of their conversation, which he instinctively knew that he would enjoy. Or, he could pack up and be home in fifteen minutes and spend a quiet evening with the dogs; much like every other evening. He shook his head, picked up the phone to order a pizza for delivery to the office, flipped the computer back on and spread his notes out on his desk. The dogs could wait a little while longer.

DAY TEN

TALK AROUND TOWN

SEPTEMBER 17TH

6:12 p.m.

bertco2: Everyone here? Sorry I'm late, my niece had a soccer match and I hadn't made it to a single game all season, so I felt obligated.

pistevo: All here. It seems that David, Doc and I all have a shared music passion and we were having a friendly debate. We seem to have a bit of a disagreement about who the truly innovative American composers are.

cintle: I appreciate all of you letting me join your little group. This looks a bit more unusual than the typical cases that find their way to my practice.

bertco2: It's less personal, which makes it much easier to be analytical in our evaluation. You finally get the opportunity to theorize on all the information absorbed from your academic days — which typically seem to fall into irrelevance when a living, breathing, human being is injected into the process.

imdoc: I agree, the people are less real — at least to everyone but Robert. In school we are all taught using case studies. It's what we are accustomed to, and where our comfort zone was originally established. The difference is that in the real world you don't just deal with the issues, but also all of the accompanying baggage. That becomes a primary factor in your actions, if not the most significant driver. You begin analyzing less, and reacting more.

pistevo: Even being here in person, the situations that I've been exposed to on a daily basis seem a bit surreal.

imdoc: Any chance to follow up on our previous conversation?

pistevo: True to form, I ran into a couple of peculiar things throughout the day. I tracked down Abe's mother again to ask her a few more questions about her husband, but once I arrived, she clearly didn't want to discuss him at any length. Her mood had decidedly turned distant toward me since my last visit. The only help she offered was that I go talk to the boys down at the Alley Cat. Apparently, he had talked more to them the last twenty years of his life than to anyone in the family.

THE ALLEY CAT

6:15 p.m.

cintle: Is that a local bar?

pistevo: Loosely speaking. It's actually more of a party store than a bar. It's about a quarter of a mile down the road from their house. The store is nothing but beer, wine, liquor and snacks. Remarkably, no staples, not even any bread or milk. However, on a positive note, you can buy a drink of anything for a nominal price.

bertco2: Is that legal?

pistevo: I've come to believe that they don't worry too much about such technicalities in these parts. Inside, the two workers, who it turned out were also the owners, had the rather peculiar customer relations approach of being completely hammered — which I learned from others around town was pretty much a permanent state. They continued to work on their condition throughout our conversation.

imdoc: Were they sober enough to offer any help?

pistevo: In spite of their condition, they were able to offer a lot of insight regarding Philip Lincoln. It seems that Abe's father left quite a lasting impression on them. It was the older of the two, who had a huge belly on a freakishly frail frame, that snapped to life when I started asking questions about him.

"Remember him, who could forget," he spat at me as he spoke. "We called him the answer man. He would come here every day during Jeopardy to buy his daily brew supply."

cintle: Jeopardy?

pistevo: Wait, this really takes an interesting turn.

"He would come in here every evening and get half tanked waitin' for the show to begin. Then, he would try to best all the contestants on the tube to the answer. We would keep track of his score, and every night that he won we would knock a buck off his bill. Of course, by the end of the show he had no idea what his tab really was."

"Did he ever win?"

"Did he ever win? It was damn odd for him to lose. May have been a drunk and a slob, but he was frickin' brilliant. Was many a night that he would answer near every question right. Never saw any of those egg heads on the show ever do that have ya?"

"I can't say that I have."

"Well, I've seen it bunches right here in this very establishment. Fact, every time he missed an answer he'd be madder than a speared pike. When he lost, stand clear, cause the man had a nasty temper. He'd start smashing bottles and thrown' whatever was in reach. We'd just stand back ringin' up the bill till he cooled down."

"Was he ever able to pay the bill?"

"Hell no, but we didn't mind. We got more than enough, and in the end, got more than the cost out of him. During show time he'd attract a group of nine or ten others down to watch who were all serious drinkers themselves. They'd all sit about waitin' for him lose on a bad night, or tell the bottles on the good nights. We made out dang good, at least good enough to keep us in business and drink, which is no small task," he laughed as he raised a brown bottle that he had peeled the label off to his lips.

"Tell the bottles, what exactly was that."

"I have to say, he had a good trick there. You could pull any bottle off the shelf and he'd tell you the story."

"What kind of story?"

"Just 'bout anything you wanted to know. He'd start out tellin' ya where it was made, and a little history 'bout the brewery or still, then go on about the town. Some history, maybe a little gossip. Like if it was some city in the South he'd tell what took place there during the Civil War. Maybe something about a Confederate officer that lived there, a nearby battle, or prison or such. Never sure how much of it was true, but it really didn't matter cause he was a good storyteller," he smiled as he talked, "and profitable," he took a swig. "He would lean against the wall, mostly with his eyes shut, swaying a bit from side to side as he spoke. Then, all the sudden, he'd get pissed at one thing or another and slam the door behind him. And with that, the show for the night would be over. Soon after, we'd be lockin' the door and headin' up stairs for the night."

"How long would all of this last on a typical night?"

"Generally, little more than an hour. Many times, less. He was more like a storm that blew in, wreaked some havoc, and blew back out. It's not the same without him, that's for certain. It's not easy to draw a crowd into a place like this."

Looking around the store I had to agree. "Why Jeopardy, did he ever give any reason?"

"He thought they was gonna call."

"He thought they were going to call him to be a contestant on the show?"

"That's right. Back when he'd been in the service he'd sent them a letter and he was just waitin' to hear back. We heard that story near every night round here for years."

"He spent his whole life waiting for a call from Jeopardy? By the time he died it had been decades since he sent that letter."

"None of us here could figure why they never rang. The guy was a real brain; he'd a broke the bank."

"Probably why they never called, too expensive and they knew it," the other partner that I thought was sleeping suddenly chimed in.

"He had the whole thing planned out. The house, the jet black Caddy; he was just waitin' for the call," the first jumped back in.

After that, I lost all control of the conversation and we digressed into a detailed discussion of how to gut a deer and where the best 'poachin' spots were that I'll spare you from.

MS. CLAUDETTE

6:27 p.m.

imdoc: Any success at making contact at the bookstore, library or gridiron?

pistevo: As far as learning anything new concerning Abe, I struck out at the bookstore, but it was worth the effort. The lone employee, Ms. Claudette, is in her early seventies and clearly couldn't see the price tags or cash register as she checked customers out. In reality, it was more of a newsstand than a bookstore.

imdoc: Just the one in town?

pistevo: Yes, and as I said, more magazines, newspapers and a coffee shop than bookstore. The proprietor, who was more than willing to engage in a conversation and ignore her paying customers, was not only unfamiliar with Abe's father, she had never heard of a single member of the Lincoln family, didn't know where the Alley Cat was located in town, and hadn't been back to the local high school since she graduated fifty-two years ago. She informed me that she had attended school in the old building uptown and wasn't even sure where the new school was located.

imdoc: At least the town has a new school. It's nice to finally hear something, anything, positive about the community.

pistevo: Good thought concerning the school, but after my conversation with Ms. Claudette, I inquired around town about the vintage of the 'new' school, which turned out to be the early sixties. But keep the faith, if nothing else, this little side track will tell you something kind about the town folk.

bertco2: Based on her lack of knowledge about the surrounding community, are we to assume that she lives somewhere else?

pistevo: Afraid not. It became obvious during our ninety minute conversation that her country place, as she called it, was less than a mile away from the store. Not only that, it's same house that she was raised in.

cintle: She never left home?

pistevo: Never left. A final note, I had a little time to kill last night, so I drove out to see where she lives, and not that anyone cares about the specifics of the local geography in these parts, but there are only six structures between her house and the store. Ma Lincoln's place and the Alley Cat are two of them. As for the high school, it's around the bend north of her house about half a mile.

imdoc: And through the years she has taken little notice of her surroundings on her daily commute; I think that's a statement rather than a question.

pistevo: Very little, but recall my earlier comment regarding her vision. The 'drive' constitutes a Honda dirt bike in the summer, and a Polaris snowmobile in the winter. As I would learn later in the day from the librarian, the good folks of the town have learned to accommodate her particular driving style, which includes not only both lanes, but also both shoulders. Monday through Saturday, she leaves her house at precisely 7:45 a.m. for the store, and then locks up and heads for home at 5:15 p.m.. Summer on a dirt bike, or if there is snow on the ground, or even in the air for that matter, by snowmobile.

bertco2: Even if there is no snow on the ground?

pistevo: As I understand it, even if it's just flurries. She claims that the dirt bike is dangerous in the snow.

cintle: I like this woman.

pistevo: Everyone likes this woman, and I understand why. The entire time she talked she said absolutely nothing of any interest or significance, yet, I found her completely captivating. A truly charming person, even if I learned absolutely nothing more about Abe's family. As one person described her, "a town treasure worthy of keeping the road clear for a few minutes every morning and evening." I would learn later that the local police officer on duty is unofficially charged with making sure that she has a safe commute to and from work each day. They also make sure that if it starts snowing during the day someone rides the bike to her house, exchanges it for the snowmobile, and then drives it back and leaves it at the store. Apparently, she never remembers what she rode in on eight hours earlier in the day.

Her means of transportation has been replaced or upgraded courtesy of the Mayor and local garage on several occasions to ensure that she has as safe a passage as possible considering her chosen modes. Not one to accept charity, her limited vision has allowed them to pass off any significant upgrades, or even replacement vehicles, as manufacturing recalls.

imdoc: Obviously, a great story, and I'm truly glad to hear something good about the community, however, I'm in a bit of a time crunch. You mentioned the library, anything new or interesting?

PRUDY

6:43 p.m.

pistevo: Sorry, back to the task at hand. I'll try to be brief and stick to the facts. Ma Lincoln visited the library every Monday morning to pick up her husband's predetermined reading materials from the librarian, Prudy. He had very strict instructions concerning what types of books he insisted on:

Five books per week, all different subjects.

Two new releases, one fiction, one nonfiction.

Additionally, one history, one science and one biography, (autobiographies, were deemed too subjective).

If two new books were not deemed 'worthy', Prudy was to use her discretion in replacing them with books from the genre of her choosing.

Prudy showed me the detailed log that she kept on her iMac, because as she put it, "duplicity was not tolerated." Putting 'not tolerated' in real terms, if she repeated a book, even years later, he would rip out the pages and give Ma Lincoln just the cover to return to the library.

bertco2: Sounds like he was a high maintenance customer.

pistevo: From what I have been able to learn, he was a high maintenance everything. But as you can imagine, he was Prudy's favorite customer. In a town where the library gets very little use, he was her weekly pet project. It was obvious from our time together that she put a lot of time each week into reading new book reviews and combing through their current inventory to try to meet his needs. I also sensed that the coffee, bagels and a couple of hours of conversation every Monday morning with Ma Lincoln was one of her weekly social highlights.

imdoc: I'm beginning to sense from the way that your story is developing that Prudy became one of your primary information sources for filling you in on the town happenings.

pistevo: She wound up being *the* reliable source of information in this town. Let me wrap this section up with a little dialog from my conversation with her, which will shed some light on what kind of person she is.

imdoc: Please do.

pistevo: Prudy was telling me that although being a librarian in a small town didn't pay a living wage, she had developed a second skill in her youth, that although unrelated, helped to pay the bills, and it was her true love.

"I grew up working in my Dad's garage fixing up old cars that he would sell in the front yard that's how I developed my love for books," she talked without using any commas or periods, so I will give it back to you in 'Prudy talk.'

"You turned to books because you disliked working in your Dad's garage?" It seemed like a logical leap to me.

"Not at all my Dad developed a very serious case of arthritis in my teen years so there were certain jobs that he simply couldn't do on those days I would work on the cars and he would sit on a stool next to me and read aloud for hours he was worried that I enjoyed fixing cars so much that I might take up the family trade which he affectionately referred to as 'white-trash-front-yard-car-sales-business' he wanted me to get an education and do something with my mind."

"Sounds like a good father."

"Great father he insisted that I get the kind of grades throughout high school that would lead to scholarships when my time came to go to college he drove me off to school and told me that if I ever quit I wasn't welcome back at home at the time it seemed very cruel but obviously he was determined that I would lead a better life than he had."

"But without you, he had lost his source of income."

"We got lucky there he landed a job driving the county snowplow he was laid off in the summer months but he had lived his whole life on very little so it wasn't a problem," she stopped to smile, which was the only time she appeared to take a breath the entire time I was there. "When he died from lung cancer — he was a very heavy smoker I learned that he had a life insurance policy that paid half to me half to the county for the establishment of a library with the stipulation that I would run it when I completed my education."

"He was going to make sure that you didn't follow in his footsteps."

"And it almost worked," she stood and motioned for me to follow her to the back of the library. "I took my half of the money and built a garage on the back on the library I work on cars during the day as time permits and when people come in looking for books which isn't very often an alarm sounds and I wander up front," that explained the librarian with the black fingernails. "Sometimes it's ideal to live in a town small enough that having an auto-repair-library makes perfect sense," she had read my thoughts. "It has allowed me to keep involved in both of my interests.

cintle: And as the local mechanic, that's where you were able to get the scoop on Ms. Claudette.

pistevo: Precisely, she does all the work on her bike and snowmobile, as well as all the local police vehicles. I finally found the person that had a rational perspective on what was going on around her.

bertco2:   Convenient for everyone involved.

pistevo: More than just convenient, it's a matter of family. Ms. Claudette was the oldest of twelve kids. Prudy's mom and the Mayor are twins, and the youngest of the clan.

cintle: Which explains why they are so much help to her.

pistevo: At least part of it.

imdoc: That's all a bit more than I can absorb right now. What about any other family members, anything interesting from Prudy, or for that matter, anyone else?"

pistevo: Interestingly, her only comments about Abe were that she found the circumstances around him to be curious. I don't think that it ever had an effect on her, so for the most part, she chose to ignore it. I did, however, find her description of Abe's uncle brief, but rather entertaining.

             "He was a nut as a child a crazy young man and grew into a senile old man well before his years."

             I haven't been able to find anyone that could think of anything redeeming about him.

cintle: That's almost as odd as the father, everyone has something good about them, no matter how vile they appear.

pistevo: I would tend to agree, but in this town I failed to find any evidence to support that theory. They seem to all have very similar, and equally very negative, emotional reactions to Lewis.

bertco2:   And of the mother, anything of her?

pistevo: Not directly, but everyone only had good things to say about her. In the end, she may have the most unique ability. She has held together a very bizarre family much better than ever could have been expected. I would imagine that was a task that consumed all of her energy.

imdoc: I tend to agree based on what you have said. We have some reasonable evidence of the exceptional abilities of the others, but her real contribution will never be fully appreciated or acknowledged.   Although, it seems to be the single practical ability of the family.

NEXT?

7:01 p.m.

pistevo: So, what does all of this tell us about Abe?

imdoc: Quite a bit, at least about his family.   Do you
            want the long or the short diagnosis?

bertco2:   Short.

pistevo: Short.

imdoc: We have a group of highly capable individuals
            who expect perfection from themselves, and
            quite naturally, fail to meet perfection.   As a
            result, a disproportionate percentage of them fail
            completely.

bertco2:   Which is not particularly uncommon, but in this
            case it has been taken to the extreme.

imdoc: Precisely, and when they weren't perfect, they
            self-destructed, and then went away and hid from
            the world.   I would say that Abe was the only
            member of the family we have seen so far that
            could deal with reality. Thus, he went on with his
            life, while all of the others continue to crucify

themselves on a daily basis.   It would also explain why he appears to have so little contact with them today.

cintle: Hopefully, Kennedy will be able to make similar adjustments as he matures.

pistevo: Does any of this tell us anything meaningful about why Abe developed such a distinct and lasting nickname? We have had many interesting conversations, and I've been exposed to people unlike any that I ever expected to come across, but I still have no answers for my client.

imdoc: The name took hold when he failed to inflict the same level of pain on himself, so others filled the void to help him fulfill the family destiny. Unnecessarily simplistic, but nevertheless, logical.   He has been referred to as SH for so long, from so many sources, that it stuck with him because it appears neither he, nor his family, made any effort to change it.   I would suggest that we concentrate more on how to shake the distinction going forward.

bertco2:   What about the people of his hometown?   Is there anything we can say about them? Do they play any part?

imdoc: I would like to pull rank here, if you will all allow me, and make a highly academic observation based on the few people Steven has exposed us to.

pistevo: Go ahead Doc, fill us with wisdom.

imdoc: I frequently find people that are exposed to very little of the 'real' world, at least as we would define it. They live in a vacuum, if you will. It's important to note that this phenomena isn't limited just to small towns; I find people from the most metropolitan of areas plagued with the same limitations. Their reference point to life is so narrow that they fail to realize the significance of others, as well as their own insignificance. However, in this case, as good as that sounds, I don't believe that would be a correct conclusion.

cintle: More likely, we are dealing with an above average percentage of idiots.

imdoc: Clinically speaking, yes. With the possible exception of our client's family, who would probably fall somewhere in the manic-depressive-self-destructive-genius category.

bertco2:   Now, there's a conclusion you won't find in too many textbooks.

imdoc: At long last I'll gain some well-deserved academic notoriety for coining a new psycho-babble category to stick people into.

cintle: I'll look forward to the articles detailing your findings.

imdoc: And, in this case, our subjects, alas, they are leaders in the community, so they are equally followed and despised. I believe that if we find a way to deal with Abe, we can initiate a domino effect that will reverberate throughout the entire town, and that can only be positive.

bertco2:   I agree. It tells us nothing about Abe, but quite frankly, I would be quick to advise him that he has done remarkably well to come from those influences with the lone scare of an unfortunate nickname.

cintle: I would be willing to bet that if you spent much time in that community you would find some close family relations.

imdoc: And years of it — I was thinking the same thing. You can't create an entire community of similar, shall we say, weaknesses, without a limited gene pool.

pistevo: So where do we go from here? The only thing that I was unable to follow up on was visiting one of Kennedy's football practices. I'm going to have to meet with Abe some time in the next week, and I would like to have one last talk with all of you before that fateful day. How about in two days around 7:00? I'm headed out in the morning, so I will have a lot of time to think about it during the drive.   Hopefully, we can develop something profound to offer.

imdoc: Great, talk to all of you then.

cintle: I should be there.

bertco2:   That's a good time for me.

DAY 11

WRAP UP

September 18th

5:22 p.m.

It had been a painfully long drive home, even longer than his trip north a week earlier because of all the construction on I-75. He had tried to concentrate on Abe's case as he made his way south, but gave up after an hour of making little progress, plugged in the Ipod, cranked up the volume, and started singing along.

Once back home, he picked up Rat from the neighbor down the block that had been dog sitting, nuked a frozen pizza, and then settled in for the evening. Tomorrow morning it was back to work, and he was finding it impossible to relax because he knew that it was only seventy-two hours until he met with Abe and his wife.

He pecked away at his laptop as he finished editing his notes. He had done the research, followed the training, uncovered an almost endless list of potentially significant facts, and yet, had no idea how to start weaving it all together in a meaningful way. He sat down, sinking deeper and deeper into frustration, when the phone rang and jolted him out of his trance.

"Hello."

"Steven, this is Jill Cochran," it took Steven a few seconds to place the name with imdoc. "Sorry to call you at home, but I have a proposition for you," she said in a voice much different than Steven had imagined. "Look, I've put together a little experiment for tomorrow night, and I was really hoping that you could take part. My Intro to Psych class is going to have a debate about your case at 6:00 p.m., and I would like to bring you in online."

Steven thought for a moment. "Well, considering that I have no idea where I'm headed with this case, it can only help."

"Don't be too hard on yourself; this is just the kind of thing I'm supposed to be trained in, and I have no clear thoughts on what the next step should be," Doc quickly replied. "Besides, irrespective of any advice we may or may not receive, it will make my students think, which is not an easy thing to do. Basically, what I try to do is trick them into it."

"Great, what do you want from me?" Steven asked.

"I'll send information out in the morning to you, Robert and David concerning where to meet us online. I will introduce you as some kind of expert, and we'll just see where it goes from there," Doc replied.

"So, do I need to prepare anything?"

"No, no, I've provided each student with an abridged version of what has taken place to date for review. I've tried to weed out all the noise to get them to concentrate on the issues. All you need to do is respond when I key you."

"Okay, that I should be able to do," Steven responded. "As long as you promise to bail me out if I get too deep in a hole, or more likely, start to look stupid."

"Promise."

"Great, I'll look forward to getting your instructions."

SEPTEMBER 18

9:41 p.m.

To: pistevo (Steven)
Cc: bertco2 (Robert);cintle (David)
From: imdoc

Good evening. I managed to get a hold of Robert and David shortly after our conversation and bring them up to speed. They will be able to watch what's going on, but you will be the only one with the ability to interact with the students.

I gave my class the homework assignment to come up with the best recommendations to deal with the SH issue, as I am calling it in class. They are to meet offline tonight in small groups and pick the four best options, which they will present to us. I will have screened them before they are presented so that I can help to develop their thoughts.

Go to site www.communityind.edu, click on class 45y2, and enter code dlc17, and you will be live. Class starts at six p.m., I'll be live a few minutes before. I don't have video conferencing, however, I can project your response for the class to see. Look forward to meeting up with you.

Jill

DAY 12

INTRODUCTION TO PSYCHOLOGY 101

September 19th

6:01 p.m.

imdoc: Steven, good to have you here. The kids are slowly wandering into class, so once I have them settled down, I will have about five minutes to review their progress before involving you in any discussion. You won't be able to see or hear what's going on, so you will just have to watch your screen until I address you.

My plan is to let the leader of each team type a brief summary of their recommendation. You can comment as you see fit. I will give my comments to the class and type it to you.

pistevo: I'm ready and waiting.

imdoc: I've gone through the format with each group, and they're ready to proceed. They are simply going to type from my screen so that the rest of the class can see their conclusions, which means that they will pop up under my name.

imdoc: We're going live in thirty seconds.

imdoc   I would like to welcome Mr. Steven Gillian to tonight's discussion. On behalf of the college and the Introduction to Psychology class, I want to thank you for allowing us to participate in your latest case. Opportunities like this are invaluable for instructors to provide students with real world challenges.

pistevo: Thanks for having me. I'm pleased to have the opportunity to share with your students.

imdoc: The first group will now come up and present their recommendation. I have requested that their suggestions be as succinct as possible.

imdoc: We tried to look at the source of the real issue. Was there a single point that seemed to be the most significant contributor to the problems that the majority of the town continues to suffer from. After a lot of arguing, none of us could come up with a single redeeming feature attributable to Coach Reed. Agreeing that our initial recommendation of having someone remove him from the human race probably wasn't a realistic academic response, we would like to suggest approaching the teacher's union and have him fired. At least that way they could limit the damage inflicted on future generations. We took this alternative because we can't see any way to go back and change what has already happened. Abe seems to be doing all right as long as he avoids his home town. The most significant step for him would be to tell his wife to start calling him by his name.

Steven waited until he was sure that they had stopped writing, then tried to respond in a way that wouldn't make him sound like he had no real experience in managing cases.

pistevo: Probably a legitimate avenue to pursue; however, by your own admission, it doesn't address my primary task of trying to separate the nickname from my client. I would also like to have Dr. Cochran's comments on the probability of getting a teacher/counselor fired after thirty plus years of service.

imdoc: Doc here, I would agree. However, some communities are more receptive to the idea of early retirement, which might prove to be a realistic alternative.

imdoc: I'm off the big screen for a moment. I realize that their plans are fairly thin, but they are providing me a basis to enlarge the discussion, so bear with me. Rather than look at each plan individually, you may see a more comprehensive possibility rise to the surface that will unfold over the next couple of presentations. It might prove to be my overactive imagination, but I intentionally had them present in the given order, hoping that we have accidentally stumbled on to a path worthy of consideration. For right now, just tuck it away. Let's continue with the second group.

imdoc: After much debate, we decided that he should simply embrace the initials SH, and tell the child that it stands for Super Hero. It would be an easy transition since that's how every kid wants to look at their parents. His wife's task would be to avoid any conversation that could lead to a discussion concerning its origins. The child, would never know the difference.

pistevo: A very good thought, my only concern would be that the child could never visit Dad's hometown without the risk of being exposed, which I suspect might make the inevitable revelation even more traumatic. The underlying issue would never be dealt with, so it would always be threatening to resurface.

imdoc: We thought of that too, and had some possible thoughts on ways to deal with it. However, Dr. Cochran wanted us to leave the idea as presented until the end of class. As usual, she's in the process of manipulating all of us — probably, including you!

imdoc: As the instructor, and the person handing out the grades, my position allows me a certain amount of academic license. On to group three:

imdoc: Group three here. Our solution may seem a little bit simplistic, however, maybe that's what is really needed here. Reinforcing what the first group said, how about starting with his wife refraining from calling him SH, and use his real name. Then, let Abe's mom know that they expect the same from her. Surely, she can't object to her child not being called Shit-Head. It would require limiting their exposure to Abe's hometown, but none of us could come up with the downside to that.

pistevo: That's a very legitimate approach. I wrestle with the fact that I may have to recommend that Abe needs to completely reject his youth, which by any normal standards, would be considered wildly successful.

imdoc: I think that is the perfect transition into the final recommendation. Group four:

imdoc: We felt that the problems around Abe, his family, and the community are too intermingled to address his issues on their own. As a result, we tried to develop a comprehensive plan. In the end, the solution seemed equally impossible yet totally obvious. We need to change history, or more importantly, at least the town's perception of it.

pistevo: I'm not sure that I understand, but I'm intrigued.

imdoc: Dr. Cochran back at the controls again. Let me take center stage here and see if I can't steer all the recommendations into a single direction using the Group Four thoughts as the foundation. Steven, you won't be able to hear, however, I will be soliciting comments from the class as I try to capture the larger concept.

pistevo: I'm not sure where you're going, but I'm already developing some thoughts of my own.

imdoc: Maybe the best thing from me to do now is go offline with my students and begin the class project of altering history, or at least the town's view of it. I think that we have something good here. How about I meet you online around 8:00?

pistevo: I'll be there if you think that you have a legitimate path to pursue. All that's missing is the how, where, when and why.

MAKING A PLAN

8:17 p.m.

imdoc: Sorry that I'm so late, this project is becoming a bit consuming.

pistevo: No problem, I was just doing a little surfing to kill time.   By the way, thanks for making me sound professional in front of your students.

imdoc: Happy to do it.   You came across very well; it will provide some credibility to your web page as your business expands.

pistevo: Good thought.

imdoc: Classes end early on Friday for me, and if possible, the Superintendent of Abe's school has agreed to sit with you and me next Saturday back up north.   He wants to discuss the details of the idea that I laid out for him on the phone over the last hour. He said that he needs a little time to think it all through.   You may find that it's a bit complex at first, but I think that you're going to like it just the same.   David can't make the trip; however, Robert will be going with us.

pistevo: I'm sure that I can find someone to trade weekends with at work as long as we're back by Sunday evening.

imdoc: No problem. We'll leave Friday afternoon, drive as far as possible, and then get an early start in the morning so that we can make our meeting.

pistevo: Where are we going to meet?

imdoc: I'm not sure yet, I'll drop you a note in the next couple of days after talking with Robert. He's volunteered to drive, so I'll coordinate the trip through him.

pistevo: I'm glad to hear that a plan is coming together. When might I expect a few more details? When might I expect anything?

imdoc: I'm hoping to lay it all out in an email to the group in the next forty-eight hours. Sorry for being so brief, but I have an 8:30 class that I'm already late for. I promise to be back with you ASAP.

pistevo: I'll anxiously be awaiting your plan.

DAY 16

THE GRAND DECEPTION

SEPTEMBER 23rd

11:32 AM

Initially, Steven had been bewildered at the absurdity of the plan as he read through Doc's notes. However, now that he had taken some time to reflect, he gradually began to become more comfortable with the concept as he saw how everything tied neatly together. Regardless, her Intro to Psychology class, in coordination with the graphic arts class, had already put a lot of work into the 'Grand Deception,' as Doc code named it. In only a couple of days, the plan had managed to take on a life of its own. Robert, Jill and David were all in, the Superintendent appeared willing to consider any plan, regardless of its improbability, and it now seemed to Steven that there was no turning back.

In the end, it had taken Doc a lot more than forty-eight hours to coordinate everyone involved and finally provide him with the details, so he was now packing his bag for the trip north that was only a few hours off, and reviewing the details at the same time. He had called Abe yesterday and rescheduled their meeting for next Tuesday, promising that he had a resolution, and requesting that he keep an open mind when it was finally presented. Now, as he looked at the outline and all the attachments that were spread out on his kitchen table, he was having a few doubts about his response. This was either the best, or the most foolish, plan that he had ever seen. Regardless, it was the only plan.

FACE TO FACE

4:37 p.m.

Steven stood in the front window of his house as Robert pulled his Volvo wagon into the driveway. He slung his bag over his shoulder, took a deep breath, and headed outside to begin the next, and hopefully final stage of his case. Robert and Jill stepped out of the car to greet him.

"Steven," Robert extended his hand. "A pleasure to finally meet you. This is Doc, Jill Cochran."

"Great to finally meet both of you. Sounds like we're in for quite an adventure," Steven said as he shook both of their hands.

"I honestly think that we can pull this off if the Superintendent cooperates, and based on my discussions with him so far, I'm cautiously optimistic," she spoke in a quick, excited voice. "I've been running through the details of the plan in the car for the last hour with Robert to bring him up to speed on what's taken place over the past twenty-four hours. Why don't you and I hop in the back seat so that I can show you some of the completed props that the kids prepared for us. I think that you're going to be impressed; it turned out even better than I expected."

"Sounds great. Remember, I've made this trip recently, and we have more time than we need to work through the details," Steven replied.

Standing in the driveway was one of those awkward moments the Internet has helped to create, where Steven realized that the people that he had developed close relationships with in cyberspace were suddenly standing before him, but in reality, were complete strangers. At that moment he also realized that he had placed his complete faith in these strangers, and that it was too late to worry about it. He would have to live with the outcome, however it played out.

"All right then, everybody in," Robert said. "My plan is to spend the night in Mackinaw City. That will leave us about a three hour journey in the morning."

SUPERINTENDENT WILKINS

He had nearly told his secretary to take a message when the first call came in. Through the years, he had learned that in his position there was a lot of downside to accepting calls when he didn't know the background. Then, throughout the conversation, he had almost hung up on three separate occasions. He was accustomed to work related nonsensical calls at all hours, although primarily they were from parents that he doubted had even spoken to their own children. However, a call from a Ph.D., suggesting that they dig up a thirty-year-old demon that he had been trying to bury on a weekly basis since taking the job, proved to be too tempting. At least it started out that way.

The Superintendent was able to go online and quickly establish the credentials of Dr. Cochran, if indeed it had been her on the other end of the line, and although it seemed a ridiculous plan that she was suggesting, it was a ridiculous situation he found himself in. His intuition told him to call her back and cancel their meeting. He only had sixteen months until his retirement, and in the first week of October the board would name his successor, his second in command, who was woefully unqualified, but he would then happily embrace his lame-duck status and immediately begin deferring everything possible. It would flow perfectly into the plans he had made five years earlier when he took the position.

He had moved up from the Chicago area where he had taken an early retirement from a school system nearly ten times the size of his current district. It had been an emotional time with the passing of his wife of thirty-four years, and shortly after her loss he had taken refuge from the world in their lake cottage, which by chance was less than a fifteen minute drive from his current office. His first morning in town he learned of the pending superintendent opening, interviewed with the board over lunch, accepted over dinner, and called his real estate agent to list his house before nightfall. Two weeks later the house sold, his son volunteered to manage an estate sale, and he was back up north settling into the lake cottage. The next Monday he had lunch with the staff and was introduced to the legend of Abraham Lincoln.

In the end, it really had very little effect on him. Although a significant percentage of the town seemed obsessed with a game now thirty years in the past, he was able to go about his duties and unwind in a job that provided a therapeutic decompression period as he adjusted to living alone and stepping away from the stresses associated with running a school system in a major metropolitan area. Keeping on track had helped him to get through the difficult days, and then begin to adjust to his new life. He grabbed his cell phone and dialed.

"Mayor Johnson," he said as he leaned back in his chair. "I have a lunch meeting on the twenty-forth that I would like you to sit in on," he could always call off the entire plan after the meeting.

MAYOR JOHNSON

The Mayor couldn't help but smile as he reflected back on the sixty-second conversation that he had just had with Superintendent Wilkins. That was all the time he needed to offer his complete and uncompromising buy-in. He was willing to throw all of his considerable weight behind any effort, regardless of practicality, to rid his town of the one blight he had not been able to overcome. Besides, where exactly was the downside in trying?

His grandfather had moved to the area as a single young man and spent many years in the forest during the lumbering era, eventually starting a mill that would come to dominate the area, and later be handed down to his father. In turn, his father had expanded the mill into a feed store and agricultural equipment business that represented the building blocks of the town, which Mayor Johnson would inherit and grow into a postcard downtown where he owned every building for the entire three blocks. His wife of forty-three years was a creative CPA that managed to carve up the businesses in ways that he didn't understand to maximize returns, and allow for not only the largest home in the county, but an ocean front condo north of Miami, a house just outside Scottsdale, and a cabin in Red Lodge, Montana. Of their five children, two were medical doctors, one was a dentist, one a college professor, and the youngest ran their day-to-day business in town since receiving his MBA seven years earlier. He never dreamed that life could turn out this well.   If only he could stop waking up every morning thinking about a noisy group of irrational citizens that dragged down his town all because of one missed free throw.

He smiled to himself; the moment of redemption was at hand.   He could feel it.   He could play a part in it.   He could make this happen.

DAY 17

THE SUPERINTENDENT & THE MAYOR

September 24th

11:58 a.m.

Doc was just wrapping up her brief summary on what had led up to their current meeting with Superintendent Wilkins and Mayor Johnson, who had been included upon the Superintendent's reflection after receiving Dr. Cochran's initial phone call.

"Unfortunately, I am well aware of the history surrounding Abe, Coach Reed and this entire dysfunctional community," Superintendent Wilkins interrupted. "The sooner that we can get Reed to retire, the sooner some healing can begin to take place and I can start dealing with issues that truly matter. Unfortunately, he refuses to leave, and I decided a long time ago that it wasn't worth a battle that I seriously doubt could be won."

"Which brings us to where we are today," Doc rose from her chair and reached into the large box they had carried up with them. "This is a Detroit Free Press sports section dated next Saturday," she slid the paper down the conference table in front of the Superintendent and the Mayor.

REVERSAL OF FORTUNE was printed in large block letters that dominated the entire top half of the paper. The two carefully read through the article that recounted the background of the historic game, detailing the final minutes, at least as Coach Reed, and presumably the town, recalled them. The article wrapped up with two computer generated models that claimed as proof that a manufacturing defect of the net, notably made in China two years before the infamous free-throw, had resulted in a perfect shot being incapable of passing though. The second drawing detailed the specific flaw in the net, and showed the ball falling through a correctly constructed net. The article went on to announce that the Michigan High School Athletic Association Committee in charge of Athletic Accuracy had reviewed the tapes and engineering data regarding the game in-depth, and was taking the unprecedented step of reversing the 1978 Class D State Championship.

Superintendent Wilkins took off his glasses and rubbed his forehead as Mayor Johnson broke out in a smile. "And I would assume that the Michigan High School Athletic Association Committee in charge of Athletic Accuracy is seated before me," Wilkins leaned back in his chair.

"Those of us involved in the investigation are unable to deny or confirm your statement due to the committee's uncompromising commitment to keeping its members out of the public eye to avoid any undue influence," Doc quickly replied.

"Well, at least I can now finally say that after years of frustration, I understand the source of the shit," a weary smile creased his face.

"Small victories Superintendent," Steven added.

"I would question if there may be an issue of copyright infringement involved with the Detroit Free Press?" Superintendent Wilkins continued, but his voice didn't sound too concerned.

"Precisely why your official participation in the festivities should be kept to that of an observer," Doc joined back in. "After all, you weren't with the school at the time of the game. It would be impossible for you to have any involvement beyond that of a fan."

"So, I can be delighted that this blemmish has been removed from my predecessor's record."

"Your, God rest his soul, deceased predecessor," the Mayor finally had something to say.

"Convenient," the Superintendent added.

"Indeed," Doc said as she unfolded a large poster made from a snapshot of Abe taken from his junior yearbook with Super Hero printed across the top.

"God rest SH, long live SH," the Superintendent quietly said as he smoothed out poster on his conference table.

"We have twenty copies that can be displayed around town," Steven said.

"Not enough," Mayor Wilkins interjected as he rose. "I want them the entire length of the parade route," he pulled a large cigar from his coat pocket, clipped off the end, and admired it as he carefully touched it off with a match. "And seeing as I have been fortunate enough to own every retail store along the downtown, I can guarantee they will all be in full view by dinner tonight," he blew out a quick series of smoke rings. "Lucky for me, the U.P. long ago took the strategic position not to participate in the Cuban embargo — purely for humanitarian reasons of course."

"Of course," the Superintendent replied as he accepted a cigar of his own from the Mayor.

"We thought that the parade should end at the gym where you can display this," Steven carefully unrolled a giant State Championship banner that would hang from the rafters.

"At which point I will give a stirring speech to my beloved community," the Mayor winked at the group and headed toward the door. "Which will culminate with me generously offering numerous incentives at my respective establishments in honor of the glorious, and long overdue, occasion."

"Are you at all concerned with issues of integrity Mayor?" The Superintendent said, although it didn't sound too much like a question.

"Rarely, it's far too complicated for a small town man such as myself to try to sort through on a daily basis. I leave that job to you," he raised his hand in a farewell jester. "Recall that we have all seen the tapes my friends; we honestly did win the game. Occasionally, justice moves in timeframes and manners of its own," he smiled. "Doctor, gentlemen, I will see you next Saturday morning, I have a parade to plan," he disappeared behind a cloud of bluish-gray smoke. "Always convenient when the entire community gathers in front of my establishments, all in the name of the common good of course," he paused. "It will be a great parade, I guarantee it."

"I had to at least bring up the integrity question," Superintendent Wilkins said.

"It comes with the job," Doc replied.

"One would like to believe that it does. The Mayor not only controls all the retail and restaurant businesses in town, the entire City Commission works for him in one way or another."

"Which means he controls both zoning and new business licenses," Steven added.

"Not to mention that the same holds true for those who sit on the County Commission," the Superintendent continued.

"Which makes him a powerful man in these parts," Steven said as he rose from the table.

The Superintendent shrugged. "However, I must admit that he deals with it better than most in his situation, at least he cares about the town and its people."

"Be thankful for small things," Robert said.

"Superintendent Wilkins," Doc continued, "I think that we can arrange the remainder of the details through cyberspace. You have a team to round up and a coach to meet with. Can you persuade him to step down?"

"It will be his finest moment. The culmination of years of hard work as he enters into his well-deserved retirement. Wouldn't it be fitting if the fine folks of this town pooled their resources and bought him a condo on a remote beach somewhere as a jester of their appreciation? Naturally, the school will have nothing to do with it."

"Superintendent Wilkins, we look forward to seeing you next week," Doc said as she rose from the table. "We have a long trip home and are eager to get started."

"Then, I will see you all next weekend for the show."

DAY 21

ABE

September 28th

7:18 p.m. - Abe

"So, that's it," Steven wrapped up his nearly hour-long presentation that the group had helped him to prepare for the Lincoln's.

Over the past few days he had slowly grown more comfortable with their plan. Now, sitting in front of them, with the props taped to the walls and laying on the floor, it once again seemed like an outrageous path.

"You really think that it will work?" Abe finally spoke up.

"Abe, have you ever paid any attention to your hometown?" His wife scooped the baby off the couch as she stood. "I think that it's a slam dunk," she smiled at Steven. "Besides, if it doesn't work, who cares, we've lost nothing and it will make for a great story."

"It's just that I have a lot to do this weekend," Abe started.

"I agree," she replied. "And it's all up north. I promise that your work will still be there Monday morning."

Abe took a deep breath. "She's right, it's time we put all of this behind us," they were the right words, but it still didn't sound like he shared his wife's enthusiasm.

"Steven, we appreciate your help. We'll see you Saturday morning." And with that, they were gone, and the final piece of the puzzle was in place.

DAY 24

PARADE OF CHAMPIONS

September 31st

12:17 p.m.

Steven, Robert, Dr. Cochran and David stood on the curb watching the parade slowly unfold in front of them. The streets were packed with what seemed like more people than the population of the town could possibly be. Even Uncle Lewis had managed to leave his shack for the morning, and now stood on the far side of the road leaning against a light pole with a thinly hidden flask at his side. Although, he couldn't have possibly appeared any less interested in the festivities taking place before him.

"So, what did Abe have to say about all of this?" David said as he watched the seventeen members of high school band march by.

"Honestly," Steven said after some reflection, "he seemed preoccupied. I'm not sure how much interest he ever had in this whole process. It appears that his only concern throughout the entire episode was trying to keep his wife happy."

"Wise man," Dr. Cochran replied. "I'm sure that you could all learn something from him."

"How quickly did he catch on that the entire event is a charade?" Robert said as he clapped for the parade's lone float, even though none of them were sure what it represented.

"Ivy league education," Steven replied. "He knew before I finished the first sentence."

"And of his wife," Dr. Cochran inquired.

"As I learned during meeting, she's a Bates graduate."

"So, I'll assume she picked up on it as rapidly as Abe."

"She may be the brighter of the two. In the vast sea of impressive intellectual capabilities, she simply had a blind spot when it came to dealing with her husband's nickname."

"Are we to assume that she's happy with the outcome?" They hadn't noticed that Superintendent Wilkins had slipped in behind their small group.

"Not only happy," Steven continued, "it was her idea to meet with the local newspaper and inform them that the Detroit Free Press had bought all media rights and that they would be given free copies of the local special edition, which in turn, they could sell for a profit."

"And so all 'real' media reporting would be controlled." Dr. Cochran added.

"And you're comfortable with that?" Superintendent Wilkins inquired.

"So it would appear," Steven smiled as he spoke. "It's also helpful that among the Mayor's assets is the local paper."

"It all appears a bit disingenuous," the Superintendent said, although he didn't sound concerned.

"Perhaps, a bit," Dr. Cochran shrugged her shoulders.

They stood together clapping as the parade crept by them to the cheers of the crowd. Next was the local Police and Fire Departments, followed by an impressive collection of antique tractors, then finally by the members of the local Harley Davidson club, which included two members on Yamaha dirt bikes and one driving a go-cart.

"Regardless, it's lovely weather don't you think? Mid-sixties and sunny. Remember to tell everyone how wonderful it is here in the fall," he paused. "I'm not only the Superintendent, but chair of the Visitor's Bureau. Ignore that it's going to snow by Wednesday." He tipped his hat in their direction and began moving down the curb for his obligatory networking.

Finally, the two vehicles carrying the people of moment slowly passed in front of them. First, the sheriff's car pulling a flat bed trailer where Abe and ten of the eleven members of the 1978 team stood throwing candy to the delighted youngsters who darted around the street in search of spoil.

"The sheriff's car has a hitch," Dr. Cochran said to no one in particular.

"And a bike rack," Robert added.

"Someone felt that the sheriff's car would represent justice finally being done," Steven said flatly.

The final vehicle was the largest Ford monster pickup truck any of them had ever seen on, or off, a road. It was complete with an impressive ladder mounted to the side that was activated by a customized remote control made from a garage door opener that operated a hydraulic system to allow for ease of entry. Coach Reed stood in the bed of the truck, a smile beaming from ear to ear, flanked on each side by two very tall young men wearing Michigan State sweatshirts.

"The meaning behind the truck?" Robert said.

"Not surprisingly, the largest vehicle of its type in the county," Steven responded. "It's supposed to symbolize that he is on top of the world — king for a day."

"And obviously a pickup truck is inseparable from that objective," Robert said as he smiled. "What of the two young men in the MSU sweatshirts?" he continued.

"Members of our community college basketball team which I managed to bribe with a free vacation inclusive of all the beer they could drink." Dr. Cochran said unapologetically.

"You're going to have to help with the relevance," David turned toward him.

"Clearly, considering that the Michigan High School Athletic Association in charge of Athletic Accuracy reversed a State Championship which in turn would have led to Coach Reed landing a job at Michigan State before their National Championship season, they would want to acknowledge such a possibility by sending player representatives from the school in support of the correcting of such a heinous oversight," she tried to look serious as the others stared blankly at her. "It made perfect sense to Coach Reed."

"So we have two tall students from your community college impersonating basketball players from Michigan State," Robert was the first to appreciate the thought process.

"Actually, they are just two tall young men wearing Michigan State sweatshirts waving to the crowd. No one has claimed that they were anything else," Steven added.

"And it's just a coincidence that they're both black. Doesn't that have a racist feel to it?" David replied as he turned around.

"Possibly at first glance it might appear that way, but I would ask you to consider my earlier comment about the free beer offer to college students. It's an offer that is completely color blind. They are both in my class this fall, so they got the nod over the rest of the team. What could possibly be less racist?" She smiled. "Besides, everyone along the parade route assuming two tall black men are basketball players is what is actually racist. It seems," Dr. Cochran continued, "that the MHSAAAA and the MSU athletic department were unable to coordinate activities of their own on such short notice, so an alternative plan needed to be implemented."

"Naturally, they are both of legal drinking age?" David replied.

Dr. Cochran turned toward the rest of the group, for the first time looking less in control, "Now, that probably would have been an appropriate question."

"I've heard of many under the table recruiting tactics; however, free beer for a weekend in the U.P. is not one I'm familiar with. You might want to buy their silence before returning to campus," Steven smiled. "Try buying them off with more beer, I understand it's an effective incentive." They all laughed quietly.

"It would seem that I need to a new plan to deal with the unintended consequences of my current plan," she shook her head. "I'll be calling you all in the morning for your thoughts."

AND, IN THE END........................

12:41 p.m.

They entered the gym just as Superintendent Wilkins was beginning what he promised would be a very short speech on his part. "At this time I don't even want to talk about the historic reversal, what it means to this community, this school, or the players standing behind me."

"He's separating himself from the entire festivities just in case reality ever comes crashing down around him," Dr. Cochran whispered. "He will just be another victim in the community."

"At this moment, I would like to focus on the man of honor before Coach Reed assumes the microphone," he turned to the coach. "It is appropriate that on this day we acknowledge your retirement from this fine establishment, and by the power entrusted to me as the Superintendent of this fine district, I am hereby waiving the mandatory waiting period and presenting you this plaque for your immediate induction into the Athletic Hall of Fame."

"He really is very good," Robert said quietly. "He never mentioned the second State Title, and yet has secured the retirement he so desperately wanted."

"In truth, Coach Reed didn't want to retire," Dr. Cochran replied. "Superintendent Wilkins persuaded him that he could use the emotions of the parade and his retirement to ignore any obligatory waiting period for the hall of fame. It could be his grand finale. In the end, it came down to Coach Reed just couldn't wait to get his hands on the plaque."

"Doubtlessly, he took a few liberties with the presentation," Steven said.

"One can only assume," Dr. Cochran replied. "My understanding is that the Mayor made a significant contribution to Coach's condo fund. Apparently, there were a number of people throughout the community that thought retirement was good, but retirement in another state was better still."

Superintendent Wilkins moved across the gym after wrapping up his speech, and then joined them as Coach Reed took center stage, tears running down his face. "So, the only question remaining is, what now?" He spoke without looking directly at any of them.

They all stood listening to Coach Reed, trying to make sense of his speech, which seemed to be covering thirty years of completely unrelated events. He was hugging the State-Championship trophy that had been given to him before the parade in one arm, his hall of fame plaque in the other, paying more attention to the hardware than the audience.

Finally, Doc spoke up. "Normal life I would presume."

The mood was broken by the sound of a motorcycle driving up to the open door and stopping just before it entered the gym. They turned in unison to watch Ms. Claudette take off her helmet, climb off the Honda, and shuffle into the gym. A City Police officer stood a few paces behind her, then stepped up and moved the bike off the sidewalk when she disappeared.

"Normalcy, or at least our version of it," Superintendent Wilkins smiled.

"Which is all any of us can truly strive for," Doc smiled. "My apologies, I felt compelled to wrap up our strange journey with something philosophical."

"I meant to tell you earlier," the Superintendent lowered his voice. "I had a staff meeting yesterday morning that included everyone currently employed throughout the school system. It is now formal policy that anyone referring to Kennedy by SF or Shit-Face will be fired immediately. All students will be given detention for using any nickname deemed inappropriate."

"A long time coming," Doc replied quietly.

"Just for a follow up, I dropped in on football practice later in the day," he smiled. "Remarkably, Kennedy's helmet now reads Special K."

"It may take some time to completely disappear, but that's the step that was needed," Robert added.

"Well done Steven," Doc whispered. "Another case solved where everyone lives happily ever after."

Steven looked around the gym. The State Championship banner was rolled up and ready to be revealed to the cheering crowd. Abe's achievements were now proudly displayed in their proper place at the top of each record board. A smaller banner with his Harvard achievements was displayed just off to the side. At the far end of the gym Abe's wife stood holding their son and was staring at him with an amused smile on her face. They gave a simple nod in the direction of each other, he patted Dr. Cochran, David and Robert on the back, shook the superintendent's hand, and turned and left the gym as Coach Reed reluctantly stepped back from the microphone and surrendered the stage to Mayor Johnson.

"None of this is real," Abe's sister Carol stood just outside the gym with a slight smile on her face as he stepped back outside.

"I think the appropriate question is, is it real enough?" Steven replied after some thought.

She looked inside the gym as it erupted in applause at the dropping of the banner. "If it helps my brother and the community, then perhaps yes, it is real enough," she turned toward him. "Regardless, it really was very clever. You fixed an event that never mattered with an event that isn't real," she turned to leave. "I left a box of my writings in your car. I'll look forward to hearing back what you think."

He slid into his car, looking at the overflowing box on the passenger seat. Nine hours home and back to normal life — or at least his version of it.